THE
NAUGHTY
LIST

Make Mine A Menage, Book 1

Jodi Redford

The Naughty List
Copyright © 2011,2017 by Jodi Redford.

Edited by Sasha Knight

Book and Cover design by Jodi Redford

http://www.jodiredford.com

CHAPTER ONE

No doubt about it. Bram Colton and Ryan Hollister were the proud owners of the hottest buns in Macomb County. No, make that the entire state of Michigan.

Mentally wiping the imaginary drool from her chin, Lacey McGuire pulled her gaze from the tight back ends of the two men in question and instead stared at the receipts piled on her desk. Unfortunately, those amazing posteriors belonged to her business partners and best buddies. Okay, and frequent stars of her sexiest fantasies, damn it. Which only made her desperate need for concentration more difficult—and necessary.

"Hey, Lace. What do you think? Better angle?"

Bram's deep baritone managed to snag her focus from the data she'd been inputting into the electronic spreadsheet. Rather than a pair of firm butts, she was met with the equally tempting visual of broad, muscular chests—one covered with a sporty navy blue Henley and the other by a hunter green flannel shirt. Both men wore jeans today, making it all too easy to notice the intriguing bulges behind their flies. Not the angle Bram had been referring to, though it was definitely fantastic.

Cheeks flushing, she lifted her scrutiny to the velvet painting of Elvis that Ry and Bram had *thoughtfully* positioned on the adjacent wall of her office. The tacky thing was her consolation prize for chickening out on their dare to sing "Like a Virgin" on karaoke night while dolled up in the accompanying Madonna getup. Like there'd been any chance in hell of that happening.

Which meant she was stuck with Elvis. For life. Or until the damn painting perished courtesy of a mysterious accident. She transferred her gaze to Bram's and Ry's smug grins and ground her teeth. "You do realize I have two voodoo dolls in my drawer that bear striking resemblances to you both, right?"

Bram snickered. "Doubt there's space left for more pins."

"Trust me, I'll make room."

His hearty laugh holding no trace of repentance, Bram ducked around Ry and opened the door to her office. Boisterous noise from the bar rushed inside the small room before Bram exited and snicked the door shut, sealing off the cacophony. Ry continued fussing with the

Elvis painting, obviously wanting to make sure she had the best possible view from her desk.

Asshole.

Despite her annoyance, her gaze lingered a tad longer than necessary on the broad expanse of his back. Although it was now covered with flannel, she'd seen it plenty of times gloriously bare. There'd been that summer three years ago, when he and Bram had worked the entire month of August at her house, installing her new deck. They'd saved her a small fortune by eliminating the need to hire a contractor, but her sanity and libido had barely survived the constant sight of Ry and Bram right outside her screen door, their tanned, buff torsos glistening with sweat from the relentless heat.

Her vibrator had burned through a ton of batteries those four weeks. If she added up the cost, it probably *would* have been cheaper to pay a carpenter.

Ry stepped away from the picture and hooked his thumbs in the waistband of his jeans. "Well, I think that looks pretty damn groovy, baby."

She squinted at him. "You did *not* just say groovy."

"I'm trying to keep in spirit with the sixties and Elvis theme." He rocked his pelvis in a dead-on impersonation of the King.

Her mouth went dry. Holy crap, those hips should be outlawed. Squirming in her seat, she scowled and returned her stare to the velvet painting. "That butt-ugly thing should take a cue from Elvis and leave the building."

"Not gonna happen, sweets. And in case you were

cooking up an evil plot in that pretty head of yours, Bram and I paid the artist extra to use flame-retardant fabric and paints."

Damn. They knew her too well.

His grin crafty, Ry plopped down onto the couch and stretched out his long legs. Faded denim pulled snug over powerful thighs, cupping that impressive package between his legs. Gulping, she tried to remember what she was supposed to be doing instead of ogling her best friend's crotch. Oh yeah. Logging last night's receipts. She scrambled for the stack and began adding the figures to the spreadsheet. All the while she was hyper aware of Ry lazily sprawled less than five feet away from her. Why oh why did he have to decide to park his gorgeous fanny in her office when her horniness meter seemed to be at an all-time high? She was about to demand that very question—well, minus the last part, obviously—when she recalled the Christmas decorations taking up most of his and Bram's quarters. Normally the artificial tree and evergreen garlands and wreaths would be out in the restaurant and not squirreled away in one of the offices, but with the big Beach Party shindig this coming weekend, every inch of the bar had been taken over with tropical-themed festivity.

Damn. She was stuck with Ry and her repressed hormones.

Maybe not jumping back into the dating pool after the fiasco with Dan, her ex fiancé, hadn't been so smart.

Frowning, she mulled over the sad state of her sex life. It'd been almost a year since she'd broken their engagement after learning that Dan had slept with the stripper from his bachelor party. At the time, she'd been devastated to the point of never wanting to put her heart through the turmoil of loving someone again. It'd taken several more months for her sexuality to return after the bruising it'd suffered, but even so, she hadn't been ready to entrust her body or heart to another man. Instead she'd relied on her trusty vibrator and made do with her erotic fantasy men— Ry and Bram. Only lately, her fantasies were constantly intruding at the worst times, making it difficult to concentrate on even the most mundane tasks.

Yes, this obsession with her best friends was pathetic. And probably unhealthy.

The lively—and incredibly annoying—opening bars of "Who Let the Dogs Out" blasted from her cell phone, announcing an incoming call from Bram. She shot a glare in Ry's direction. "Is it your guys' mission to make work impossible for me today?"

Ry lifted his linebacker-sized shoulders in a negligent shrug. "Maybe he misses you already."

She snorted before returning her attention to her computer monitor. Ten seconds later, her cell chirped as a text came in. Fingers flying over the keyboard, she gave Ry another peeved look and he laughed.

"Why am I getting the evil stare? *He's* the one bugging you."

"Probably because *you* put him up to it." It'd always

been that way. Ever since high school, there hadn't been a dare Ry issued that Bram didn't feel challenged to take on. It was for that very reason the three of them became friends. As a teenager, she'd been gawky and shy. Okay, as an adult, she wasn't much better, but at least the braces were history. During their sophomore year, Ry had gotten it into his head to bet Bram that he didn't have the balls to partner up with her—the smartest student in class—during chemistry lab. Seeing how Bram had always tended to be the class clown who thought homework was a four-letter word, Ry had been justified in his assumption that she would tell Bram no way. Little had Ry counted on Bram pulling a fast one on him by offering her ten bucks to partner up. They became the three amigos shortly after that. There were still days when she wondered what weird cosmic alignment sandwiched her in the middle of Bram and Ry—two of the sexiest playboys gifted to womankind.

Her cheeks burned as the word *sandwiched* tumbled around in her brain, inciting a host of naughty and provocative images. It wasn't the first time her mind took that particular fork in the road. A hot, wicked threesome with her best buds was her most frequent fantasy. Who knew how many explosive orgasms she'd shuddered through while imagining Bram buried balls deep in her pussy as Ry's cock pumped away in her ass. Or vice versa.

Just thinking about it now was enough to make her clit throb with anticipation. She smothered a groan and shifted in her chair, the soft wool of her slacks a tormenting friction on her inner thighs. The damp, clinging state of her panties shuttled a hot wave of embarrassment through her. Oh God. She was soaking wet and on the verge of orgasm—while one of the starring leads of her fantasies sat across from her, completely clueless of her predicament.

Ry's nearness only added fuel to her fire. Although she knew she'd regret it, she risked a peek in his direction. He'd leaned back and rested his head on the top of the small tweed couch. His eyes were closed and his features relaxed, but she didn't think he was asleep. Last night's late shift was no doubt catching up with him though. Usually Donna, the evening manager, covered closing, but a nasty bug had put the woman out of commission the past few days.

Taking advantage of Ry's unawareness, Lacey drank in his delicious masculinity. Dark stubble shadowed his strong jaw. It'd been a few days since he'd shaved. She loved him like this—sexy, with a rough edge. Here was the dangerous lover from her dreams. The man who controlled her body with one smoldering look and made her climax with one husky command.

Come.

Her clit tingled in response to the phantom whisper in her head. She squeezed her thighs together, the ache increasing. In her mind, Ry's dusky eyelashes fluttered open and his heated gaze met hers. She knew he saw her naked need, her struggle to keep the looming orgasm at bay. The glint in his whisky-brown eyes informed her of the implausibility of avoiding the inevitable. Furthermore, he'd be the one to push her over the edge.

He lifted to his feet and walked to her desk, his presence overwhelming her senses, invading her space. His focus lingered on the tight buds of her nipples apparent beneath her sweater before drifting down to the V of her thighs. "Are you wet, baby?"

She tried to look away, but his adamant stare held her firm. Wouldn't allow her to hide from him. She bit her lip and nodded.

"Show me."

Anyone could come in and see her. How could she expose herself—in every sense of the word—to that possibility? Illicit excitement raced through her veins and sped up her pulse, making her dizzy and breathless.

"Do it, Lace. Let me see how much you want me." Ry's hand stroked over the impressive bulge tenting the fly of his jeans.

There was no way she could deny him. Or herself. Her fingers shook as she eased down her zipper and slowly revealed the first inch or so of her red silk thong. A satisfied growl rolled from Ry. "My favorite."

That's why she'd worn it. She knew how much he loved the texture of the silk against her skin. And *he* knew how much she loved it when he pulled the fabric snug between the cheeks of her ass, using the tormenting friction to tease her clit and labia, knowing full well the addition of his fingers applying pressure on the bunched elastic riding against her puckered rosebud would be enough to shoot her over the edge. But he never went that easy on her. No, he was a master at prolonging her pleasure. Keeping her suspended on the precipice of orgasm for endless hours.

The tension in his big body and the promise in his sinful eyes hinted she was in for a long night. "Take your pants off, Lace. Panties too."

"But—"

"Now." The firmness in his tone thrilled her. He'd find a delicious way to punish her for disobeying him. Of that she was certain.

She shimmied from her slacks and thong. Ry dropped onto his haunches and picked up her underwear. He buried his nose in the garment and inhaled with a lusty groan. The sound, along with the expression on his face, made her skin flush and her clit ache.

"Christ, you smell fucking good, Lace. I want to lap you up." His knuckles whitened as his grip tightened on the slip of scarlet silk. "But first I want to watch you play with that pretty little pussy for me."

She whimpered and he grasped the edge of her chair, swiveling the seat sideways until she faced him fully. He tugged her closer so her butt rested on the edge of the padded leather. His warm, calloused palms slid along her inner thighs, refusing to touch her exactly where she wanted him most. He hooked her knees over the arms of the chair, opening her completely to his gaze. Cool air stirred across her wetness. A lush decadence spiraled within her. Under Ry's hot, watchful stare, she was free to be as uninhibited as she pleased. There was no awkwardness, no shame. No worry that he would think her anything less than what she was.

A vibrant sex goddess.

The intensity in his eyes and the prominent tic in his jaw banished her ever-present doubts. There was also the massive erection straining at the placket of his jeans to consider. With fantasy Ry, she never questioned if he desired her. No, he wanted her. Always. Any way, *every* way, he could have her.

"You're dripping, baby. And your clit is all swollen and glistening. I think you better rub it. Make it feel good for me."

"But I want you to lick me."

"I will. I'm plannin' on spending all night eating out your sweet pussy. But I want you to strum that clit first. Get it nice and juicy for me." He reached for her hand and sucked her index finger into his mouth, wetting it. She didn't require extra lubrication, but the rasp of his tongue and slight scrape of his teeth was beyond arousing. A fresh surge of moisture trickled from her slit and slid toward the crack of her ass. Ry released her finger and guided it to her pussy. Her clit throbbed, begging for her touch, but she bypassed the demanding nubbin and grazed the slick folds of her labia, teasing herself. And Ry. His nostrils flared, his consuming focus glued to her motions. Undulating her hips, she dragged her fingertip higher in slow increments.

She hovered just beneath the quivering bundle of nerves, waiting, stringing out the torment. Ry licked his lips, his erection thickening.

Unable to deny herself a second longer, she caressed her clit. The contact shot an electrical current of pleasure throughout her body, making her jolt. A moan snuck past her lips. "Ooh."

Ry's attention jerked to her face. His gaze locked with hers. "Tell me what you're feeling."

She'd known he would ask. Ry was always all about the details. "My clit is wet and slippery."

"Is it beating beneath your finger?"

"Not yet. Soon."

"Tease it with little flicks." A hungry hum of pleasure rumbled from Ry's chest when she complied with his request. "You like that, don't you, baby?"

"I like your tongue on me more. Or your cock. Inside me."

A sexy, knowing smile tipped one corner of Ry's mouth. "Maybe. But we both know what you like best."

She tried to look away from his dark, seductive stare, but it reeled her in.

"What is it that you love most, Lace?"

"Y-you. Fucking me."

"Where?"

"In my ass." She bit her lip.

"What is Bram doing while I'm fucking your ass? Watching?"

She shook her head. "He's with us. Filling my pussy."

"That's right. We're fucking you together, baby. The way it's always been meant to be. Our cocks are pounding into you, soaked with your juices."

A strangled groan tore from her throat, the first beat coursing through her clit.

"We're gonna make you come, Lace. So fucking hard."

Lacey's phone chimed again. She gave a startled jerk, snapping from her fantasy. *Holy shit.* Her breath sawing from her lungs in short gasps, she dropped her gaze to her lap, half afraid she'd find her hand buried between her legs. She was relieved to note that it wasn't. Mortifying enough that she'd been mentally masturbating at work. If she'd been pleasuring herself in reality? She would have crawled beneath her desk and not come out for the next week, particularly if Ry had opened his eyes and noticed what she'd been up to.

Reminded of her fantasy lover's presence, her focus veered to the couch. He was still in his relaxed pose, and the unmistakable sound of soft snores proclaimed him asleep.

Thank God for small miracles.

Her cell beeped again, announcing yet another text. There was no great mystery as to who it was most likely from. Smothering a sigh, she swiped the aggravating device from her bag and glanced at the words typed on the screen. *Why aren't you rescuing me?*

She skipped to the previous message. *Olivia's got me cornered in the bar.*

Lacey blew out a heavy breath. Olivia Barnam was only one among a long parade of bimbettes who'd fallen into Bram's bed, but the woman had proven to be less willing to leave it than the others, and as a result, had gotten into the habit of stalking him at work. While she wasn't exactly a fan of Olivia's, Bram was a big boy. Let him take care of his own damn problems. She punched in a quick reply. *Busy right now.*

Almost immediately, Bram's response pinged back at her. *I'll do anything you want. Just. Get. Your. Ass. Out. Here.*

Anything she wanted? Her pussy grew even wetter as she considered the possibilities. Yeah, not bloody likely. She eyed the wall before quickly typing in her selling price. *Elvis. I want him destroyed.*

Bram's answer took a little longer coming this time. *Ry won't go for that.*

Sucks to be you, then. A spark of orneriness prompted her to add, *Give Olivia a smooch from me.* She hit send. Before she even lowered her cell to her desk, Bram's message flashed across the display.

Fine. Elvis is adios.

Ooh, yeah. Victory tasted sweet. She scooted out of her seat and strode to the door. A moment later she left Ry's snores behind and entered the Dockside's bar area. Although it wasn't technically happy hour yet, the space was already getting crowded. She spotted Bram over by the pass thru, his smile strained as Olivia plastered her sex-kitten body against him. Wow, he hadn't been exaggerating about being cornered. Olivia had literally backed him into the wall.

Lacey's irritability vanished. Big boy or not, Bram had been forced into an untenable situation. He couldn't very well make a scene in front of everyone, and Olivia damn well knew that.

Anger roiling in her stomach, Lacey crossed the room. As she neared, Bram looked her way and caught her eye. Relief scuttled across his gorgeous face. Elbowing her way to his side, she plunked her hands on her hips. "I've been looking all over for you. Did you forget you were supposed to help me look for the extra case of pilsner glasses?"

Bram took his cue in stride and, with an overabundance of exuberance, slapped his hand on his forehead and grimaced. "Damn, I did. Sorry."

Holy crap that was some bad acting. No wonder he was kicked out of the drama club. And here she'd always assumed it was because he'd been caught buck-ass naked in the costume changing room with Allison Reedy.

She wagged a finger at him. "Sorry's not going to cut it, Colton. I'm getting a little tired of constantly covering your butt."

Bram's eyes widened. Apparently he'd read between the lines. Good. He needed to either learn how to handle his bimbettes better, or keep his dick in his pants once in a while.

Olivia's smile should have come with a frostbite

warning. "Bram and I were in the middle of a conversation. He'll have to help you later."

Lacey blinked before narrowing her eyes. Oh hell no. *The bitch did* not *just undermine me in my own damn restaurant.* "No, I need him now." Amazingly, she managed to keep her voice level and calm.

Flicking one long, platinum strand of hair over her shoulder, Olivia swept Lacey with a disdainful glance. "Please. We both know why you really came trotting over here."

It was on the tip of Lacey's tongue to say, *Yeah, to save my best friend from Stalkerella.* Frankly, she didn't care if the truth pissed off Olivia, but like Bram, she didn't want to draw any more attention than they had to. "I'm afraid you'll have to enlighten me there."

"We've all seen the way you drool over Bram. And Ryan." Olivia's high-pitched laugh was more headache inducing than a kennel full of yipping Pomeranians. "As if you'd have the slightest chance, honey. You couldn't even keep your fiancé's attention for long, could you?"

Lacey's face went hot as fire before becoming icy cold. It was a strange sensation. She dimly heard Bram's low, furious baritone reprimanding Olivia, but the damning words were already out there, hovering in the air like poisoned darts.

"You know why Dan left, don't you? Because you're boring. A goody-goody who doesn't know the first thing about how to please a man. Or keep him happy." Olivia's obnoxious, tinkling laugh floated free. "Or should we say keep him *period*?"

Lacey didn't bother correcting the misstatement about Dan being the one who left. It didn't matter, and Olivia sure as hell didn't care. Bitter acid sloshed in Lacey's tummy, burning her esophagus. She swallowed, desperate to keep it down.

"I told you to shut. The. Fuck. Up." Bram's rugged, handsome features held a wealth of rage as his fingers dug into the powder blue cashmere covering Olivia's arms. The woman's heavily made-up eyes widened. Obviously she'd never experienced the full scope of Bram's temper.

That made two of them. In the fifteen years she'd known Bram, Lacey hadn't seen him lose it like this either. He'd always been the eternal goodtime boy. Full of light and laughter. In every way Bram was the polar opposite of Ry. He was a jokester and all-around ham, whereas Ry exuded quiet intensity. Even in looks the two men would never be mistaken for twins. Besides standing a good three inches taller than Ry's solid six foot one, Bram had the sun-kissed, blond surfer-god vibe working for him in spades. Ry, on the other hand, looked more suited to a Harley than board shorts. Though God knows, he filled those out mighty fine too on the rare occasions he donned a pair.

But now Bram appeared to be getting in touch with his inner alpha. "If I ever hear you talk to Lacey that way again, so help me, I can't be held responsible for my actions. *Comprende*?"

Olivia gulped before nodding vigorously.

"Glad we have that clear. Now how about you leave before I have the bouncers escort you out?"

Her full, bottom lip turning down in a pout, Olivia curled her fingers around Bram's forearms. "But I drove here specifically to see you. I've missed you, Brammy Bear."

Brammy Bear? *Oh barf.*

"I'm not telling you this again. We're no longer together. Don't waste your time or mine anymore." Not waiting for Olivia's reply, Bram shouldered past her and grabbed Lacey by the elbow. He hauled her toward his and Ry's office, his pace brisk. With her shorter legs, it took two steps to his one to keep up with him. He shoved open his door and followed her inside the cramped space before securing the lock to guarantee their privacy. The overwhelming, pungent smell of plastic greenery and cinnamon-spiked pinecones floated around them. Bram tunneled a hand through his spiky hair. "Shit. Lace, I'm sorry. Olivia's an idiot."

"It's not your fault she's a moron." They both knew that wasn't what he'd been apologizing for, but she couldn't bring herself to acknowledge the real reason his expression looked agonized and uncomfortable.

Unfortunately, Bram didn't feel so inclined. "She doesn't know what the hell she's talking about. You're not boring. Or a goody-goody. Dan was—*is*—a damn fool for what he did."

"I know that."

Bram stared into her eyes, apparently not completely buying her assertion. "Lace, you're a desirable woman. Any man with half a brain wouldn't do anything to fuck up his future with you."

She gave a crooked smile. "Well there you go. Dan did have half a brain. Too bad he carted it around in the wrong head." Not giving Bram an opportunity to voice any further pearls of wisdom, she turned toward the door and wrestled the lock open. She had to get out of there before she gave in to the tears prickling at the backs of her eyelids.

"Lace—"

She escaped the office and sealed off the remainder of Bram's words by shutting the door behind her. Praying no one noticed her fierce trembling, she dashed toward the restrooms.

CHAPTER TWO

"I'm going to kill that damn Olivia."

Ry rubbed the grogginess from his eyes as Bram snicked Lacey's office door shut. It was a miracle Bram hadn't slammed it, judging from the way he white-knuckled the knob. Ry cracked a yawn. "What'd psycho Barbie do now?"

"She brought up Dan. In front of Lacey."

Ry stopped in mid-stretch. A growl slipped past his throat. "She did *what?*"

"She insinuated that the engagement ended because Lace was boring."

"You've got to be shittin' me." He gave his head a shake. "Jesus, Olivia is one stupid broad." It was beyond him what Bram had seen in her. Well, other than the obvious—enormous tits and legs that didn't know the meaning of the word shut.

"You'll get no argument from me there. I kicked her

ass out and told her to stay gone. For good."

Ry nodded. "Where's Lace?"

"She ducked into the women's restroom." Bram's eyes clouded. "She looked like she was seconds away from crying when she hightailed it away from me."

Ry swore beneath his breath. It was a damn good thing Olivia had heeded Bram's advice and not stuck around. Because she sure as shit didn't want to cross Ry's path right now.

Bram parked his butt on the arm of the couch. "Do you think we should send one of the waitresses to check on Lace?"

He met the agonized uncertainty in Bram's eyes. No doubt it was a mirror of Ry's own expression. Desperate as he was to ensure that she was okay, he remembered the pain Lacey went through following her decision to break her engagement. Most folks had been kind and sympathetic to the situation. But there'd been those who'd whispered and snickered behind her back. She'd tried her best to hold her head high and pretend those gossiping fuckers meant nothing to her. But he'd known better.

"No, we'll give her a minute." He wouldn't draw any nosy attention to Lacey's predicament if he could help it.

Bram nodded solemnly. They were silent for a long stretch, the tension slowly escalating with each tick of the wall clock situated near the Elvis painting. The uneasiness percolated in Ry's gut. What if Lacey had taken off? She was in no condition to drive, not as upset as she likely was.

He glanced toward her desk and noticed her purse was still on the floor. Okay, one problem solved. She couldn't go anywhere without her keys.

Even as he processed the thought, the door swung open and Lacey walked inside the office. Her eyes looked red and puffy. *Motherfucker.* His chest vising, he leapt to his feet and wrapped her in his arms. He sensed her struggle to hold in more tears but eventually a soft sob escaped, nearly muffled by his shirt. Running his palms in soothing circles along her back, he kissed the top of her head. Bram stepped to the other side of Lacey and rubbed her trembling shoulders before also ducking and kissing her temple.

She sighed, accepting their comfort. Her hand clutched his waist, the other reaching for Bram. She snuggled close, her breasts pillowing against Ry's chest. The delicious floral scent she always wore clung to every inch of her. Even her honey-blonde hair seemed to be infused with the luscious essence that was Lacey. The aroma invaded his senses, adding its own brand of torment as he reeled under the heady intoxication of her.

Christ, would there ever be a woman who affected him the same way as Lacey? Doubtful. God knows he'd searched all these years to find another to cure him of his obsession with the woman in his arms. He'd found plenty of willing participants more than happy to warm his sheets, but not one of them made his heart beat faster or left him woozy with punch-drunk love. A million times he'd wanted to make Lacey his, stake his claim. But he couldn't.

Because of the man across from him. Bram.

Almost from the moment they'd both laid eyes on Lacey, they'd fallen hard. There'd only been one time he and Bram ever raised fists to each other. It happened the day they finally came clean about their feelings regarding Lacey. Being young and arrogant, Ry had fully expected to kick Bram's ass, even though his best friend clearly held the advantage of additional height and muscle. But Bram hadn't backed down. It'd infuriated Ry, until he realized the reason for Bram's stubbornness. Bram was just as crazy about Lacey—he would have fought to the death for her. The knowledge had acted like a kick to the balls. For them both.

There was no way either of them could be the bigger man and step aside. Which left them only one alternative.

Neither one of them could have Lacey. Not if their friendship held any hope of surviving.

So for the past fifteen years Ry and Bram kept their hands to themselves. And suffered the biggest case of blue balls known to mankind. Something that Ry was all too familiar with at the moment. He angled his hips away from Lacey, not wanting her to notice the rising state of his erection.

Son of a bitch. He felt like a giant dick—no pun intended. Here she was devastated and crying her eyes out over that fucktard ex of hers. Definitely not an ideal time for Ry to be sporting the mother of all boners. He glanced at Bram and noticed that his best friend was wearing a wry grin. No doubt he was dealing with a similar predicament and could empathize with Ry.

Lacey sniffled and swiped a hand over her cheeks. Juvenile as it was, Ry couldn't help the flash of satisfaction that streaked through him over the knowledge that she'd let go of Bram but not him. She looked up at Ry, those beautiful blue eyes swimming with the remnants of her tears. It took every ounce of his control not to lean down and kiss her. Properly. No chaste peck of his lips on the crown of her head, but a full-on devouring of her mouth. That luscious mouth he'd imagined wrapped around his cock countless times.

Somehow he snuffed his groan before it could give him away. He was without a doubt the biggest asshole alive to be lusting over Lacey like this. She needed friendship and a healthy dose of comforting. His damn dick would just have to stay the hell out of the equation.

She patted his waist before shuffling out from between him and Bram. "Okay, I have no idea why I let any of this upset me. Dan is ancient history, for Pete's sake."

Thank God for that too. When he and Bram had found out about what that motherfucker did, they'd paid Dan a visit and gave him a good ass kicking. The shithead was lucky they didn't do more than break his nose and bruise a few of his ribs, as well as his ego. It'd been mighty tempting to shatter the bastard's kneecaps for making Lacey cry. It was beyond incomprehensible to Ry why any man would cheat on her. Christ, Lacey was a walking wet dream. All she had to do was smile—hell, *breathe*—and he was close to busting a nut. She'd starred in thousands of his raunchiest and sweetest late-night fantasies while he was lying in bed, his dick so hard it could hammer nails. Half the time he didn't even need to stroke his cock for it to shoot off like a cannon. The mental image of Lacey riding him, her wet pussy gliding along his length, was always enough to do the trick.

It wasn't strictly a sexual thing either. Hell, he could handle that, even if it made him crazy and turned on more often than he cared to be. No, the really damnable part was how fucking in love he was with her. Other than Bram, there wasn't anyone in this world that he felt as close to as he did Lacey. Unlike his two best friends, he hadn't been raised in a traditional household. An abusive dad forced him to run away from home at a young age. Child protective services had stepped in and shuttled him off to various foster parents until an estranged uncle took him in when he was ten. Life became relatively normal after that, but it wasn't until he met Bram and Lacey that he truly felt a part of a family. *Their* family. Yeah, it was probably weird to look at his two best friends in that light, but so be it. Becoming business partners and going in together on the purchase of the Dockside cemented their bond as the three amigos. The only possible way his life could be happier was if Lacey's heart belonged to him.

He might ache for something more, but he'd have to be content with her friendship. Even if it was all he'd ever have, he was still a damn lucky man to have that much. Yeah, Dan was a fool for destroying his future with Lacey. And all for a silicone-enhanced, easy lay. The reminder of the fucktard brought Ry's thoughts back to Lacey's recent meltdown. He hugged her close again and massaged the nape of her neck. "It's only been a year, baby. Plenty of folks need more time than that to heal."

"Sure, if they're grieving the loss of someone."

"Do...do you miss Dan?" *Please God, let her say no.* The idea of Lacey still carrying a torch for that asshole sat like an elephant on Ry's chest.

Lacey's face scrunched in an adorable way. "Absolutely not. He had his chance and blew it."

My sentiments exactly. Frankly, he'd never thought Dan was good enough for her to begin with. Sure, the guy seemed decent at first glance, but there'd always been something that rubbed Ry the wrong way. He'd originally thought it was his jealousy over Dan having unfettered access to Lacey's bed and her heart. Two things that should rightfully belong to Ry, damn it. But once the news of Dan's unfaithfulness spread, Ry had figured out what had been poking at the edges of his conscience regarding Dan. The guy had never looked at Lacey with the light of love shining from his eyes, or like he'd die tomorrow if she were ever taken away from him. Even when he'd been getting his ass kicked by Ry and Bram, Dan hadn't once stopped his pathetic whining to ask if Lacey was okay and somehow surviving the heartache he'd put her through. That was just wrong in Ry's book. A man didn't put the woman he loved through that kind of pain and turmoil. He was supposed to cherish her. Beat to a pulp anyone who dared to hurt her.

Lacey stepped away from him again and fidgeted with the charm bracelet hooked around her right wrist. It was a gift he and Bram had given her several Christmases ago. Every year they tried to outdo each other coming up with the perfect charm to add to the collection. Bram got the biggest *ooh* and *ah* last year by popping for a sterling-silver turtle with emerald chips inset into its shell. Damn dickhead. This Christmas Ry would have to pull out all the stops if he didn't want to get left in the dust.

Lacey stopped her fussing and offered them both a hesitant glance. "It isn't so much about Dan as the possibility that I've...lost my mojo. If I even had it in the first place."

He blinked at her. "What are you talking about?"

She swallowed, the muscles in her throat working. "M-maybe Olivia has a point. About me being boring."

It took more willpower than he swore he possessed not to punch a hole in the wall. Or yank Lacey into his arms and slam his mouth over hers, proving without words precisely how damn ridiculous Olivia's statement had been. "Baby, no way in hell are you the slightest bit boring."

"You're my friend. You're supposed to say that." She dropped her hands with a resigned exhale.

"No, I'm saying it because it's true."

She gave him her patented stare that always let him know when she thought he was being deliberately obtuse or stubborn. "I think we all know that I'll never be mistaken for a stripper."

Oh Jesus. Is that what this was about? "Please tell me you're not comparing yourself to a stripper right now," he growled, furious that Lacey's confidence had been undermined to that degree.

"No. I know I'm not...sexy like that."

He and Bram coughed at the same time, but Bram was the first to recover his voice. "Lace, you are."

She rolled her eyes. "Hello. Did you not hear what I said about the friend thing?"

"Just because we're friends doesn't mean I don't find you sexy." There was no mistaking the slight huskiness underlying Bram's confession.

Lacey's cheeks turned pink and she averted her eyes. "Bram, please. We've all seen the women you've dated. They could be supermodels." Her lips twitched into a mischievous smile. Just the sight of it was enough to give Ry wood. "Make that supermodel strippers in the case of Stalkerella Olivia. Regardless, I'm nowhere near their league."

"Yeah, you're miles beyond it," Bram pointed out adamantly. "In another universe, practically."

Ry couldn't agree with him more. Lacey returned to Bram and stood on tiptoe to kiss his cheek. Ry tried not to let the jealousy eat at him.

"You're a good friend," Lacey whispered to Bram

before dropping back onto her heels. She glanced over at Ry. "You both are."

Oh yeah? So how come he didn't get a goddamn kiss? He sent the obnoxiously grinning Bram a mulish glare as Lacey paced between them.

"But the truth is I can't keep leaning on you guys to boost my sagging confidence. If I want to reclaim my mojo, I'm going to have to suck it up and..." taking a deep breath, she took several steps back and faced them both, "...jump into the dating pool."

Ry could feel his heart knocking in an erratic rhythm. Lacey...dating? Someone other than him? He'd barely survived her engagement to Dan. How the fuck would he get through this? Without consciously thinking about it, he turned his stare on Bram. His best friend wore the same panicked look.

Fuck yeah. They were both screwed.

CHAPTER THREE

By the time she finally dragged herself home, Lacey was dead on her feet. She plunked her purse onto the front end table and shrugged from her down-filled jacket. After hanging the garment in the closet, she rolled her shoulders, attempting to work out the kinks. A glass of wine sounded spectacular at the moment. Precisely what she needed to help her relax and wind down for the night.

She slipped off her suede snow boots and left them to dry near the heat register before traipsing into the kitchen. She poured the Pinot noir into her glass and took a sip, her gaze traveling to the stark landscape on the other side of the window. The snow-capped frozen surface of Lake Saint Clair resembled a glittering, crystallized desert. The barrenness of a Michigan winter never failed to depress her and make her long for the summer months, when the lakes were sparkling and sailboats and freighters bobbed in the distant waves.

After she'd broken her engagement to Dan, she'd briefly considered putting her house up for sale and moving south. Somewhere along the Atlantic coast, so she would still have her water views to enjoy. But there'd been the restaurant to consider, along with her family and Ry and Bram.

Especially Ry and Bram. The idea of leaving and only seeing them on occasion had made her stomach cramp to the point she'd felt physically ill whenever she thought about it. Even before they'd purchased the Dockside three years ago, they'd rarely gone longer than a few days between seeing each other. Since then, they'd become inseparable.

So she'd stayed put and muddled through.

Damn it, she was sick of muddling through. It was way past time to start living again. Getting her groove on and having a little fun. And maybe even some sex. She gulped down another sip and nodded. "Yeah, that's right. I'm going to have sex, damn it. With an actual person." She drained her glass and topped it off. Her brain was starting to feel fuzzy. Probably she shouldn't have any more to drink.

That's something a boring person would think. The taunting whisper in her head was enough to convince her to slurp through a couple large swallows of wine. A warm glow steadily crept through her veins. Tightening her grip on the glass, she swiveled away from the counter and journeyed down the hall to her bedroom. She even put a little sashaying hip action into her walk. More than likely she looked silly and uncoordinated as a one-legged duck, but with no one around to judge, she didn't give a hairy rat's behind. She settled her wineglass on the nightstand and shimmied out of her clothes. It was definitely a flannel jammies evening. But as she reached for her favorite pair—the ones with snowboarding kangaroos—the mocking voice floated through her mind again.

I bet Olivia doesn't wear pajamas that have marsupials on them.

The thought managed to add an extra layer of acid to the wine sloshing around in her stomach. Though she tried to push the doubts away, they started piling up again. She stared at the flannel garment in her hands, her heart growing heavy.

Who was she kidding? She was so far from being sexy, it was ridiculous. Men weren't interested in women like her—the average girl next door who was passably pretty but nothing to rave about. They wanted the flash and sparkle of someone like Olivia. The type of girl who stopped men in their tracks and caused multi-car pileups every time she crossed a street.

Her mood taking a steep downward slant, Lacey pulled on her pajamas and slumped on the edge of her bed. More than anything, she wished she was more like the woman she portrayed in her secret fantasies. *That* Lacey was lusty and uninhibited. She had two gorgeous hunks filling her days and nights with indescribable pleasure. They thought she was beautiful. A sex goddess worthy of worship.

Fantasy Lacey would do anything and revel in every hedonistic moment.

What would I do if I was her? All the time. Not just in my mind? She picked up her wine and took a fortifying gulp. Would she have the nerve to let go of her fears, even if it meant exposing a side of herself that left her feeling vulnerable? If she were willing to risk it all, what *would* she do?

With that intriguing question spiraling through her mind, she rushed to the dresser and grabbed her laptop. Too often she did accounting work from the comfort of her bed. No doubt yet another thing that boring people did all the time.

Snipping off that unhelpful thought, she snuggled into the pillows and powered on the laptop. With the screen's backlight giving her courage in the dark, she opened up a fresh document and formatted it to create a bulleted list. She typed in the number one and stared at the blinking cursor for what seemed an eternity. "Oh for Pete's sake. How difficult can this be?" Very, apparently.

She closed her eyes, trying to concentrate. Instead, an image of Bram flashed behind her eyelids.

Just because we're friends doesn't mean I don't find you sexy. This time when he said it, he tugged her into his arms and followed up the statement with a brain-frying kiss. Plus he was naked.

Hell, this was her fantasy. If the stud muffin insisted on clothes being optional, who was she to argue?

"Yeah, you love it when I'm nekkid, don't ya, darlin'?"

She opened her eyes. Fantasy Bram sat next to her, wearing nothing but a grin. She swept her gaze over the velvety bronze skin stretched taut over those acres of rippling muscles before zeroing in on his mouthwateringly erect cock. The rigid shaft thickened at her perusal, jutting toward her in invitation. She licked her lips. "Mm, can you blame me?"

He nodded toward her opened laptop. "Whatcha doin'?"

Her fingers fidgeted on the keyboard. "You'll think it's silly."

"No way." He scooted closer and nuzzled the side of her neck. "C'mon, you can tell me."

"I-It's a list." She gasped when Bram's tongue began slowly tracing the shell of her ear.

"For groceries?"

She shook her head, trying to focus. It was damn difficult with the way he was sucking on her earlobe. God, his oral skills were out-of-this-world extraordinary. "Not exactly."

"Then what kind?" His hand slid beneath the hem of her pajama top and caressed her tummy. Wicked fingers flirted with the elastic waistband of her bottoms.

She bit back a moan. "A...a..." She shivered as Bram's other hand ghosted up along her rib cage and cupped her breast.

His thumb brushed her nipple. "A what?" he prompted.

It took a moment to remember what they'd been talking about. "A naughty list." She had no idea where the description came from, but now that it was out there…yeah, it was definitely fitting.

Bram chuckled. "A naughty list? Sounds right up my alley." He rolled her nipple between his thumb and forefinger, making her arch into him. "So what's on it?"

"N-nothing yet."

He made a tsking noise. "And after all the inspiration Ry and I have given you?"

"I guess I'm not as creative as I thought." *That's because you're—*

As if he'd sensed the negative voice in her head, Bram scrunched her top upward and latched onto her other nipple. His teeth imprisoned the tender nub, holding it hostage to the voraciousness of his agile tongue.

God, the man knew how to use that particular organ. Okay, he wielded the one farther down south with incredible skill too. He ceased his torment for a second and glanced at her. "Get to work on that list."

"But—"

"Now, Lace. Or I'll stop."

Damn, did he know how to play some hardball. She reached for the laptop again and settled it next to her. "Number one…" She pondered the entry as Bram resumed playing with her nipples. An answer flew to her, so perfect it made her gasp. Okay, the sound might also have something to do with the luscious things Bram was doing with his mouth. "I'd sing 'Like a Virgin' at karaoke."

Bram grunted. "How the hell is that naughty?"

"I'd do it naked."

A sexy growl rumbled against her damp flesh. "*Fuck.* Yeah, gotta admit that's damn hot."

"Number two." She chewed her thumbnail, thinking. "I'd...pleasure myself."

Another chuckle came from Bram. "You already do that, darlin'. A lot, I might add."

"Nice of you to point that out," she grumbled. "And for your information, I'm intending to do it this time in front of someone else." *Holy crap. I am?* But it was so...naughty. Well, okay. That was pretty much the whole point. "Moving on to number three."

"How about you let someone tie you up and fuck you? Maybe even throw in a blindfold."

Her clit tingled at Bram's suggestion. She'd read about bondage games in a few of the erotic romances she loved. Those scenes never failed to get her juiced up. She ruffled her fingers through Bram's short spiky hair. "I knew there was a reason I keep you around."

He stopped his feasting on her breast and slid a smoky look in her direction. "My dirty, brilliant mind isn't the only reason you keep me around." He hooked his fingers into the waistband of her pajama bottoms and inched them down. After flinging the rumpled garment aside, he settled between her legs, his broad shoulders bracing her thighs open. His warm breath puffed against her soaked pussy. "Number four?"

"Sex in a public place."

One of his eyebrows arched. "Bold."

"Too much?"

"Fuck no. Just right." His tongue gave a barely there flick across her clit. She squirmed, desperate for more. He moved away, his hazel eyes teasing. "Number five?"

"I'd visit that sex club downtown. The one you think I don't know you and Ry have gone to."

His jaw dropped. "How the hell did you find out?"

"I heard you and Ry talking about it once." She blushed. "I wondered what you would do if I showed up there."

Those sinful irises darkened. "We both know the answer to that. I'd toss you over my shoulder and carry you into one of the private rooms so I could bury myself deep in your pussy for the rest of the evening."

She licked her lips. "Next up—anal."

"Don't worry, I'd give this sweet ass plenty of devotion too." As if to verify his statement, Bram ducked his head and traced the crease of her ass with his tongue before rimming her puckered opening.

Her breath lodged in her throat and stars danced in her vision. "I—I was referring to number six. Not that this isn't nice."

"Goes double for me, darlin'." Bram eased a finger into her back passage. "You'd let a man fuck you here?"

"Y-yes. If I felt comfortable enough with him."

Bram's stare bored into her. "Would anyone else be

there while this guy is balls-deep in your tight ass?"

She knew what he was asking. What he wanted to hear. "Yes," she said on a whisper.

"Number seven?"

She swallowed, her fingers shaking on the keyboard. More than any of the others, this entry terrified her the most. It was one thing to fantasize about it. Typing it would somehow make it real and force her to spring the closet door on her deepest, darkest fantasy.

"You have to do it, Lace." Another of Bram's fingers stroked inside her pussy. It moved in countermotion to its partner. "Type the words and set yourself free."

Oh God. Could she do it? Admit the one fantasy that'd sustained her for as long as she could remember? Trembling, she stared at the screen on her laptop. Words, just words. It meant nothing when she'd be the only one who ever saw them. She dragged in a deep breath and expelled it slowly. "I'd have a threesome with Ry and Bram."

"Good girl." The finger inside her pussy curved against her G-spot and rubbed determinedly. Bram's mouth closed around her clit and sucked with firm, demanding pulses. He knew exactly what it took to trip her over the edge.

The orgasm crashed into her, making her shudder and gasp. Her pussy and ass milked Bram's fingers, the quakes rocking her. All the while, Bram continued devouring her. Hungry, lusty groans vibrated against her flesh, telling her he was aroused just as much by his oral love fest as she was. Knowing how much he enjoyed going down on her only heightened her own pleasure.

The climax lasted forever, yet ended too soon. By the time she came to her senses, fantasy Bram had vanished, leaving her limp and sated.

And completely alone.

She always felt sexually satisfied after one of her solo sessions. Tonight was no exception. But this time she felt empty too. Awesome as the fantasy was, it would never be the real thing. She needed to come to grips with that.

Rolling onto her side, she stared at the list she'd created on her laptop. She started to hit the delete button, but the mocking voice paid a return visit to her head.

Goody-goody two shoes. That's all you'll ever be.

Gritting her teeth, Lacey hit save. Just to prove that her inner tormenter had her pegged all wrong, she sent a copy of the file to her work email so she could add to the list tomorrow.

"That's right. Who's the damn goody-goody now?" A spark of triumph banishing her earlier glumness, she logged off and returned the laptop to her dresser before flicking off the lights. As she climbed back into bed, one certainty flashed through her mind.

Tomorrow would be the first day of a new and naughty Lacey.

CHAPTER FOUR

Bram pulled into his parking space outside the Dockside mere seconds before Ry's Ford F-250 slid to a stop in the adjacent slot. Surprisingly, Lacey wasn't there yet. Usually she beat them to the clock every morning. Then again, she'd had a rough day yesterday. The reminder of the role Olivia played in it made Bram see red all over again.

He knew part of the reason Olivia had been such an insensitive bitch was because she'd always been jealous of the tight friendship he and Lacey shared. One night when she'd gotten stupid drunk, Olivia had slurred accusations about Lacey lusting after him. God, if only Olivia knew the truth. The only one guilty of a major case of lust was him. For Lacey.

Sometimes he wondered if he hadn't made a huge mistake agreeing to the pact with Ry about keeping their distance. With the bombshell Lacey dropped yesterday about dating again, this more than qualified as one of those times. How could he stand by and not do everything in his power to convince her to make him one of her eligible candidates?

There'd been more than one occasion when he'd debated the wisdom of him and Ry not just pouring their hearts out to Lacey and letting her decide if she could see herself with one of them. Yeah, it'd kill him if she picked Ry. But eventually one day he'd get over her, right?

Sure, maybe in my next lifetime. Blowing out a heavy breath, he cracked open the door of his Subaru Outback. An arctic blast buffeted the side of the vehicle, making the door rattle in his grip. Concerned the gust might decide to take off with part of his car, he clambered out and slammed the door shut. He reached the Dockside's entrance just as Ry did. Bram wedged his key in the lock and pushed the door open. He let Ry take care of hitting the lights in the main section of the restaurant and went to check things in the kitchen. The astringent smell of disinfectant and industrial-grade floor cleaner announced that the janitorial crew had been through and worked their magic. A note was taped to the cooler door. More than likely the supply list from Kevin, the head chef.

Bram strode to the cooler and grabbed the note. He'd give it to Lacey so she could add the items onto their weekly shopping list.

The reminder of Lacey brought his thoughts spinning back around to her adamancy about dating again. Yeah, wanting to keep her safely out of reach of some faceless dude certainly made him a selfish bastard. She deserved to find her happily ever after.

He wished to hell it would be with him.

His fist tightening on Kevin's note, Bram stalked toward the office he shared with Ry. The lights were already on and Ry was busy clearing some boxes of ornaments off his desk. Bram tossed the list on top of a stack of unopened mail and stared at the back of Ry's head. "We can't let her do it."

"What choice do we have?"

It came as no surprise to Bram that Ry knew precisely who and what he'd been referring to. When it came to Lacey, they'd always been of the same mind. Well, mostly. "We can damn well tell her how we feel."

Ry pivoted toward him, his eyes hot and his features haggard. He looked like shit. Probably hadn't slept an iota last night. That made two of them. Ry slammed his arms over his chest. "Brilliant idea, Colton. I'm sure she'd love having to choose between her two best friends. Assuming she'd want either one of our asses."

"True, but what if she ends up dating another dickwad like Dan? Are we supposed to stand by and let her get hurt all over again?"

Ry glared at him, obviously pissed by the question. "You damn well know I'd cut off my own arm before letting that happen."

"There's an easier, less drastic option than that."

"We're not making her choose." Ry bit off each word with deadly precision.

In the back of his mind, he knew Ry was right. It wouldn't be fair to foist that kind of decision on Lacey. And he valued her friendship too much to risk losing it. Still, the idea of watching her with another guy—someone who wasn't *him*—made him sick inside. "It's killing me, man."

"I know."

He stared Ry down, knowing full well that the anguished frustration in his best friend's eyes was a match to his own. "So what do we do?"

"We support Lacey. Be there for her." Ry sat down in his chair and rubbed the back of his neck. "It's what we've always done and will keep on doing."

Having no argument for that, Bram cleared a path to his own desk and powered up his computer. He slid Ry another look. "For what it's worth, if she did choose you, I'd be okay with it."

Ry cocked an eyebrow. "Really?"

Despite the heaviness in his heart, Bram grinned. "Well, first I'd wipe the floor with your ass, but yeah, eventually I'd come to grips with it."

Ry was quiet for a moment. He gazed at his keyboard, his dark eyebrows slashed low. "Guess if I had to step aside for anyone, I'd prefer it to be you." He fiddled with his mouse. "But don't go getting any ideas. Our traps are staying shut, understood?"

"Fuck, you're a stubborn asshole." Grumbling, Bram clicked on his email icon. He nearly groaned when he saw the number of new messages waiting for him. "How is it humanly possible to get two hundred new emails overnight?"

Ry grunted. "Bet you twenty bucks half of them are from internet porn sites."

Bram chuckled. "Nah. I use my personal webmail for that shit." He turned his head in time to catch Ry rolling his eyes. Returning his focus to the screen, Bram scanned down the column. "Ah damn. Maybe I spoke too soon. There's one here called The Naughty List." He moved the cursor to the delete button. Just as he was about to click it, he noticed who the sender was. "Wait, nope. It's from Lacey."

"She sent you something called The Naughty List?" There was no mistaking the disbelief in Ry's voice.

"Yeah. Looks like she forwarded it from her home email. Must be a dirty joke or something."

"From *Lacey*?"

Bram mentally tracked back to the reaction she'd given to his joke a couple days ago about the two hunters and the porcupine. "Okay. Probably not." No longer able to contain his curiosity, he opened the file attachment and waited for it to download. Once it did and he read the top line, he choked on a stunted cough.

"What?" Ry demanded. "*Is* it a dirty joke? No fucking way."

"Uh, not exactly." Blinking a few times, Bram continued to the next numbered line. What he saw there made his mouth go drier than the Sahara. "What. The.

Fuck?"

The casters on Ry's chair creaked as he pushed to his feet. "Obviously I've got to check out whatever it is."

Bram spared him the briefest glance. "Yeah. You do." By the time Ry reached his side, Bram had read down to number five. Shock might have numbed his brain, but his cock was hard as a damn baseball bat. After a few seconds of rapt silence, a colorful swear word sprang from Ry. Bram shot him a glance. "Which one are you on?"

"Three."

"Oh yeah. That one's good. But wait until you get to..." He broke off as he suddenly picked out his and Ry's names down toward the bottom of the list. His pulse speeding up, he concentrated his attention on that particular bulleted line. It took three times of reading it over to convince himself his eyes weren't playing tricks on him. Once the reality seeped into his brain, his heart hammered so hard, he actually felt a little woozy. It was tempting to pinch himself and verify that he wasn't dreaming. Or trapped in some alternate dimension. Beside him, Ry was frozen like a statue. It didn't take much to figure out that he'd finished the entire *list* too. Bram swallowed. Hard. "She wants to have a threesome. With you and me."

Ry's jaw worked but no words immediately sprang free. He cleared his throat. "There is *no* fucking way Lacey sent this."

"Dude, it's from her personal email."

"A hacker?"

He gave Ry a dry look. "One who'd know to add your and my names? Not to mention the sex club?"

Ry scowled. "How the hell does Lacey know about that?"

He shrugged. "Damned if I know."

Ry combed his fingers through his hair, his hand unsteady. "I'm having a hard time wrapping my head around this."

"Buddy, that makes two of us." He returned his attention to the monitor. It was insane—the notion that the whole time he and Ry had been lusting after Lacey, she'd been engaged in some pretty raunchy thoughts herself. About them. Holy shit. Like a moth drawn to fire, he visually devoured the last line again. His cock thickened even more. "What are we going to do about it?"

Ry's gaze jumped to him. "What do you mean *what are we going to do about it?* Nothing, goddamn it."

"We've done it before. With that woman a few years ago at the club." Just the reminder of the night in question made Bram's cock bob against his fly. He'd participated in a few threesomes before that incident, and even one afterwards, but none of them came remotely close to rocking his world like that night. It wasn't that he was secretly gay for Ry or anything. Hell, handling any cock other than his own wasn't his idea of a good time, but there was no denying that sharing a woman with Ry had been mind blowing.

"That's different. Neither of us was in love with that woman."

"Yet it was still hot and amazing."

A muscle ticked in Ry's jaw. "Your point is?"

"Imagine what it would be like with Lacey, since we do love her. It'd be out of this fucking world."

"She's not someone to just play around with."

Bram bit back a growl. "You think I don't know that? I'm not suggesting anything that she obviously doesn't already want." He waved his hand toward the computer. Indecision warred in Ry's eyes. Bram knew when to push his advantage. "Don't you see what this means? It's our shot at *both* of us being with her. She wouldn't have to choose."

"You honestly would be fine with Lacey fucking us both?"

Fine? The mental picture of being buried in Lacey's pussy while Ry shafted her ass had Bram so damn hard, he was seconds away from coming in his pants. "Yes. Aren't you?"

Tension bracketed Ry's mouth. "I don't know."

Desperation clawed at Bram's chest. He had to make Ry see reason. To believe this could work. He tapped his finger on the computer screen and read out loud, "I'd have someone blindfold me before tying me up and fucking me."

The muscle twitching grew more pronounced in Ry's jaw, and his nostrils flared. Bram knew he had his best friend by the short hairs. "Tell me you don't want to be the one doing that to her."

"Damn it. Of course I do." The gruffness in Ry's voice didn't mask the underlying hunger in his tone.

"Then I think our mission is clear." Bram gave a slow, triumphant smile. "This Christmas, we're helping Lacey check off every item on her Naughty List."

CHAPTER FIVE

It wasn't her alarm clock that snapped Lacey from a deep snooze, but rather the loud, obnoxious droning of her next-door neighbor's snow blower. Groaning, she rolled onto her back and winced as tiny pinpricks of pain lanced her temples. Oh man. Having that extra half a glass of wine had been a huge mistake.

Cautiously pulling her hand away from her eyes, she peered toward the window, where she could make out flurries of snow whipping against the glass.

What time was it, anyway?

Careful not to wrench her neck, she glanced toward the alarm clock on the nightstand. And yelped when she read the display. Nine a.m.! Why didn't the damn alarm go off? Not wasting time to investigate the cause, she jumped out of bed and scurried into the bathroom. She wasn't one of those business owners who catered to the idea of rolling into work whenever she pleased. She believed in setting a good example for the employees. In return, she liked to think they respected her work ethics. Quickly disrobing, she hopped into the shower. And promptly got pelted in the head with the bottle of shampoo that insisted on falling out of the caddy.

It was going to be one of those kinds of days.

Fifteen minutes later, she jumped into her car and dialed the heater to full blast in order to defrost the windshield. She huddled in her seat, her teeth chattering along with "Jingle Bells" on the radio. It occurred to her that she should probably call Ry and Bram to let them know she was on her way in. She rifled in her purse for her cell phone and somehow jabbed herself with a ballpoint pen. "Damn it."

Finally she latched onto her phone and pulled it free. She must not have turned it off last night because a text message waited on the display.

Girl, WTF??? Call me as soon as you get this.

Frowning, Lacey checked to see who the sender was. Jana, Bram's sister. She started to hit reply, but the clock on the dash brought her focus back to her current dilemma. She stared at the tiny peek holes that the heater had managed to create on the windshield. This was going to get her nowhere fast. Heaving a frustrated breath, she tossed the cell into her coat pocket and grabbed the ice scraper from the backseat. Several minutes later, the front and back windshields were cleared and her butt and legs were completely numb from the frigid temps. She scrambled back inside the relative warmth of her

Pathfinder and roared out of her driveway.

The Dockside was less than seven miles from her home, which was particularly nice on days like this, when the weather was crappy and she was running late. She parked next to Ry's truck and rushed toward the entrance. As she reached for the door handle, her bladder decided to pitch a fit. She squeezed her legs together. "This is what I get for sleeping in."

Her gait awkward, she hurried inside the restaurant. Ry and Bram were standing by the bar, deep in conversation. They stopped and stared at her. She waved a hand and continued streaking toward the rear hallway.

"Lacey, we need to talk." There was a strange tension in Ry's voice.

"Sorry, but my bladder is outshouting you right now," she called, beelining for the restrooms. She ducked inside the women's room and dashed into one of the stalls in the nick of time. Her relieved sigh echoing in the cramped space, she flushed and went to wash up at the sink. While she was rinsing the suds from her hands, her cell phone started ringing. Hitting the sanitizing blower with her elbow, she dug with her free hand into her coat pocket and pulled out her phone. "Hello?"

"Girl, what the *fuck*?"

It was Jana. Clutching the cell to her ear, Lacey moved away from the dryer so that she could hear better. "Is that your phrase for the day?"

"It will be if you keep sending me kinky emails."

She frowned. "Kinky emails? What are you talking about?"

"Your Naughty List. What else would I be talking about?"

Naughty...

The blood slowly started to drain from Lacey's head.

"Why didn't you tell me you were thinking about having a threesome? That's so *hot*. Okay, so I'm trying not to think of you with Bram. Because that's just a little too weird. But Ry? Day-um. Sign me up."

Oh. My. God. How...?

Frantic, Lacey replayed the events of last night. She remembered forwarding the file to her work email. Why did it go to Jana?

Unless...

Oh sweet Jesus. Did she accidentally send the email to a contact list rather than herself? Her email account had an autofill feature that she was usually pretty good about catching, but the damn wine she drank last night had definitely left her brain fuzzy. She racked her mind, trying to think of what directory started with the same letters as her name, one that would include Jana in the list. The answer slammed into her. Her "lame laughs" directory—appropriately titled because everyone on it had the same cornball sense of humor as her and appreciated the silly articles she occasionally found online and forwarded on. If that was the case—and it sure as hell looked like it—it meant everyone in that particular directory got the file. The contents of her stomach gave a dangerous lurch.

"Lacey? You still there?"

"I've got to go. I'll call you later." She hung up before Jana could protest. Her palms were so clammy, the cell phone nearly slipped from her hand. She shoved it into her coat pocket and collapsed against the wall. Her face alternated between icy cold and blistering hot. The blower had ceased its thunderous noise, making the pounding *whoosh* inside her head all the more apparent.

There was no way this was happening.

Only it was.

The good news was her "lame laughs" contact list was woefully small. Besides Jana, the only other people on it were...

Oh. Shit.

Her belly roiled and she pressed a shaky hand to her mouth.

Ry and Bram.

How was she ever going to look them in the eye? She swallowed down her nausea. Even though she knew it was pointless, she darted her gaze around the bathroom, looking for a possible escape plan. One that would miraculously teleport her to her car so she could make a quick getaway. Preferably to Hawaii, or some other destination far, far away from here.

A thought occurred to her in mid panic attack. Maybe Bram and Ry hadn't seen the email yet. If not, she could hack into their accounts and—

Lacey, we need to talk.

Her heart sank as Ry's tense demand spun in her mind.

They'd read the email. She couldn't fool herself into believing otherwise. Just like she couldn't fool herself into thinking she'd get out of the conversation waiting for her on the other side of the bathroom door. Sucking in a deep, fortifying breath, she pushed away from the wall and prepared to face her best friends.

Two men who now—without a question of a doubt—knew she wanted a kinky threesome.

Yeah, this wouldn't be awkward. At all.

The desire to race back inside the restroom stall and have a mental breakdown—or throw up—was overwhelming. Somehow she found the fortitude to take a shaky step toward the door. Then another. *You can do this, damn it.* She stepped out into the back hallway. The restaurant was eerily quiet. It was easy to pretend that she was the only one in the entire building.

If only.

Shoving her hands into her coat pockets to hide their trembling, she walked into the main bar area. Ry and Bram hadn't moved an inch from their posts. They both watched her as she approached, their expressions unreadable. That, more than anything, disturbed her. She'd half hoped Bram would be grinning and cracking lewd comments about how she'd pulled the world's biggest prank on them.

Prank...

Wait, maybe that's how she could get out of this—by

convincing them it'd merely been a bad joke. It was a long shot, considering the incredibly personal stuff she'd included on the list, but maybe they'd take pity on her and let it go.

She offered the guys a tentative smile. "Sorry about that. You know us women and our tiny bladders." She winced at her overly cheery tone. *Why am I talking about bladders?* Trying not to feel like the biggest moron on the planet, she cleared her throat. "Anyway, you wanted to speak to me about something?"

Ry stared at her for a long moment, his eyes dark and intense. She couldn't remember ever having been under the full power of his focus like that. It took every ounce of her willpower not to shiver. Or duck and hide behind the bar. "Why didn't you tell us, Lace?"

Although it was pathetic and ridiculous, she decided to play dumb. "Tell you what?"

Of course Ry wouldn't let her off that easy. "You know damn well what I'm talking about. Your threesome fantasy."

She forced a laugh. "Oh. *That.* I thought you guys would get a chuckle over it. I only wish I could have seen your faces when you read the email." Not that she'd needed to be there. It wasn't exactly difficult to conjure twin expressions of stupefied shock.

Actually, the shock she could handle. It was the inevitable pity concerning her delusional fantasy land that had her stomach in knots.

Bram sidled up next to Ry. A frown marred his features. "It was a...joke?"

"Well, duh. Of course." She rolled her eyes for good measure. "I can't believe you both fell for it."

For a brief moment she swore Bram looked disappointed. Ry, on the other hand, just leveled her with his patented let's-cut-through-the-bullshit stare. "It wasn't a joke. I know it and you know it."

"Don't be silly. Do you think I'd tell you all of that embarrassing stuff if it was *real*?"

The rugged planes of Ry's face softened, but the heat in his gaze didn't abate. "There's nothing to be embarrassed about."

"I—I didn't say I was embarrassed." Oh crap. Yes, she did. She really needed to learn how to choose her damn words better. She cleared her throat, figuring it was past time for a fast recovery. "Why would I be embarrassed over a joke?"

"Because it isn't one. But judging from how flustered you're acting, I'd say it's a safe bet you didn't intend for Bram and me to ever know about any of it. And that's really unfair of you, Lace."

The accusation in Ry's stare was almost unbearable. A thick ball of shame wedged in her throat. She'd always been brutally honest with him and Bram before, hadn't hidden anything from either of them up until now. But there were some things you didn't go blabbing to your business partners, for God's sake—like the desire to be tied up and blindfolded for a night of raunchy sex. "C-could we just forget any of this happened?"

"It's too late for that, Lace. You can't expect us to pretend we don't know. To not wonder." Ry stepped closer, his gaze drifting to her mouth. Hunger burned in his eyes.

Her heart thumped in response. She'd imagined that particular look on his face countless times, never believing she'd see it in actuality. This had to be a dream. Or another of her fantasies. The last part of his statement registered and she blinked. "W-wonder? About what?"

"You. Us." His knuckles brushed the underside of her jaw, tipping it ever so slightly upwards as his head descended. "This." The husky word feathered her lips, a prelude to the lush pressure of his mouth upon hers.

Disbelief and pure giddiness combated inside her while one startling thought spun through her brain in a ceaseless loop. *RyiskissingmeRyiskissingmeRyiskissingme.* His tongue coaxed past her lips and glided over hers, the sensation drowning out the delirious chorus in her head. He tasted of coffee and aroused male. It was the most delicious combination of all time. Even as she was reveling in that fact, a pair of hands slid around her hips from behind. Bram's heat blanketed her back. There was no mistaking the hard ridge of his erection nudging her tailbone.

This can't be happening. But even as she was trying to assure herself of that, Ry reluctantly broke their kiss and leaned back. Their gazes crashed into each other for a moment before he glanced over her head at Bram. Some unspoken communication passed between the two men. Still dizzy from Ry's kiss and confused as hell, she craned her neck to look up at Bram. Without warning, his mouth staked its own claim, taking over where Ry's had left off.

Her senses reeled from the unexpected double whammy. Getting the daylights kissed out of her by Ry was incredible enough, adding Bram to the mix...it was a damn miracle she was still standing upright. As if her body was looking to change that status quo, she swayed, her knees threatening to buckle. Bram freed one hand from her waist and tunneled his fingers through her hair, managing to hold her steady and at the same time tilt her head for better access to her mouth. His tongue was just as insistent as Ry's and possibly twice as bold.

A gruff, slightly irritated cough issued from Ry. Bram released her, his tongue taking its time to depart her mouth. Dazzled, she licked her lips and attempted to form a coherent thought. "I—I don't understand. What's going on here?" She'd been certain they'd be freaked out by the email. Having them all but devour her was the last reaction she'd been expecting, for damn sure.

Bram caressed her hip. "We want to give you that threesome, Lace. Along with everything else on your list."

Shock and a hot wave of arousal careened through her at Bram's declaration. She panned her stare between him and Ry, taking in the twin expressions of determination on their flushed features. In her mind's eye, she pictured the three of them naked on her bed, living out the fantasies she'd barely been brave enough to commit to typewritten words.

Panic began to set in. A fantasy was one thing. Actually exposing herself—in every sense of the word—to her best friends was a whole other matter. She swallowed past the words sticking in her throat. "I think that would be a bad idea."

Bram frowned. "Why? We thought that's what you wanted. Your email..."

"Was something you were never supposed to have seen." She gave Ry a sheepish look. "Yeah, you were right about that much."

"I also told you there's no going back now that we know." Ry brushed her hair away from her cheek. His fingers lingered on the side of her neck, the warmth of his touch creating pleasurable tingles.

Despite her firm resolve to ignore the sensation, she still shivered. "I don't want to ruin our friendship. Not to mention the business we've created here."

"Neither do I."

"Same goes for me," Bram echoed, squeezing her waist.

She battled the desire to lean into Bram's tempting embrace or to snuggle into the hand Ry still had curved around her nape. Instead she took a fortifying breath. "Then it's better not to risk it, right?"

"At one time I would have agreed with you." Ry's focus lowered to her mouth. His irises contained enough heat to stoke a campfire. "But now that I've kissed you, tasted you, I'm not willing to settle for what-ifs. I want to explore the possibilities beyond friendship, Lace. And I know Bram does too. Maybe it's time to stop playing it safe and just see where this takes us."

He made it sound so...reasonable. Like giving in to this insanity wouldn't inevitably result in a big crash and burn for the three of them. The knowledge that he seemed far less freaked out than her about the idea of a threesome stirred her suspicions. "Have you guys done this sort of thing before?"

Ry's gaze flicked toward Bram. "Not exactly."

She scooted out from between them and crossed her arms over her chest. "Either you have or you haven't."

Bram's broad shoulders lifted with a resigned inhale. "There was a woman. One time, Lace. That's all."

She gaped at him. His answer probably shouldn't have stunned her, particularly considering how he and Ry frequented that sex club in Pontiac. Maybe threesomes were old hat to them. No bigger a deal than going on a double date. Rather than reassure her, it only reinforced how out of her league she was with all of this. She took another step back and rubbed her arms. "I don't think I'm cut out for this."

Ry walked forward, a challenge glinting in his eyes. "How can you know if you don't try it?"

She nibbled her bottom lip, uncertainty gnawing inside her. "If this goes bad, there might be no recovery for us."

"It won't." Ry pulled her toward him, his palm curving low on her tailbone. He'd held her many times before, but the intimacy in his touch now was nearly as overwhelming as his kiss earlier. And undoubtedly that's what he'd intended, to get under her skin and storm her defenses. "We've always been the three amigos. That'll never change." His voice held an unwavering determination.

She peered into his eyes, desperately wanting to feel the same confidence he did. Bram approached and took her free hand, twining their fingers together. "Give us a chance, Lace. We'll prove to you that it'll work."

Temptation beckoned, strong and persistent, but she wasn't ready to completely throw caution to the wind. As it was, her heart pounded out of control with the compromise she was about to suggest. She was terrified at the prospect of it, but she suspected that she'd never forgive herself if she didn't at least dip her toes into the forbidden waters. "O-one item on the list. If any of us feel even the slightest bit weird about everything, it ends there, understood?"

Both men smiled, obviously convinced the outcome would be in their favor.

"Deal." Ry leaned down and brushed his lips over hers, presumably sealing the agreement. He lifted his head and his lips tugged upward. "But Bram and I get to pick the item."

She opened her mouth to protest just as Bram squeezed her left butt cheek, making her squeak instead.

Voices came from the vicinity of the kitchen, announcing that the cooks had arrived to begin prepping for the day. Ry and Bram immediately released her, but not before offering her matching stares that smoldered.

Her mouth went dry even as her pussy became unbelievably wet.

Oh God, what have I just gotten myself into?

CHAPTER SIX

Ry glanced at the clock hanging over the bar as he listened with half an ear to the story Hank Lewiston—one of the Dockside's regulars—was regaling him with. Fortunately it was a tale seventy-eight-year-old Hank was fond of recounting, meaning that Ry had heard it more than a few dozen times and could easily recite it himself if the need arose.

He couldn't remember being this anxious for a workday to end. Of course, being treated to the occasional glimpse of Lacey for the past eight hours and remembering the soft texture of her lips beneath his and the wet, tentative glide of her tongue only amped his torment and made him hard as stone.

If anyone had told him before today that he'd be itchy with anticipation over the prospect of sharing Lacey with Bram, he'd have accused them of being fucking crazy. While he did wish he'd be going solo on this seduction, the truth was he'd take Lacey any way he could have her. If that meant agreeing to a package deal, so be it. At least it would be with Bram. There'd be no damn way he could watch any other man sinking his cock into Lacey and not want to rip their balls off. Plus it helped having that previous experience with Bram. He knew what to expect, and in an odd way, they worked pretty well as a team when it came to pleasing a woman in bed. Shannon—their one-night stand—sure hadn't complained. If anything, she'd been disappointed when he and Bram declined her offer of another future rendezvous. But he and Bram had gone into it knowing they didn't want to make it permanent. There'd been no sense in leading the woman on. So they'd happily parted ways that night, and he'd been convinced it'd be a fond memory never to be repeated. Certainly not with Lacey.

Despite his best efforts to pay attention to the rest of Hank's rambling tale, Ry's thoughts wandered to the upcoming evening. He and Bram had come to the same conclusion that they needed to get the ball rolling fast, before Lacey got cold feet and changed her mind. He knew how she tended to overanalyze things. If they gave her even a day to mull the situation over, she'd find a million more reasons to talk herself out of it.

He intended to do everything in his power to keep that from happening. He wasn't averse to using all of his sexual wiles to seduce her into this threesome, and he knew Bram was more than game too.

As if the man in question had read Ry's mind, Bram

stepped into view at the opposite end of the bar and gave a subtle nod toward the rear hallway. Taking the hint, Ry clapped the back of Hank's shoulder. "Hold on a sec. I've got to go check on something in the kitchen."

Hank shrugged before shifting in his stool and transferring his attention to the unsuspecting guy in the neighboring seat. Feeling a little guilty for unwittingly foisting Hank on the poor dude, Ry escaped the bar and strode in Bram's direction. He met up with him outside the men's john. "Did you talk to Lacey about meeting us over at your place?"

"No, she's been avoiding me like the plague. Every time I went into her office, she dredged up some excuse to be somewhere else."

Ry grunted. "She can't hide forever. Why don't you grab takeout from the kitchen and head home to get everything ready? I'll work on Lacey."

"Don't let her duck out on you."

When it came to going after what he wanted, Ry could be like a Rottweiler scoping out a juicy porterhouse steak—one determined sonofabitch. There was nothing in this world he wanted more than Lacey. "Not a chance."

Bram grinned. "Maybe I should stop by Jana's place first and pick up some handcuffs. They might come in handy tonight. In more ways than one."

Bram's sister owned Wicked Delights, a lingerie store that also stocked some interesting adult novelties. Ry's cock thickened behind his fly as he pictured Lacey stretched naked on Bram's bed, her wrists cuffed to the posts and her lips wrapped around Bram's dick while Ry buried himself balls-deep in her pussy.

Fuck. Smothering a groan, he covertly adjusted himself. He must not have been as discreet with the gesture as he'd assumed because Bram cocked an eyebrow, his smirk widening.

"So is that a yes on the handcuffs?" Bram chuckled. "Hell, she did say she wanted to be tied up. Almost the same thing."

"We might have to save that for another night. She's probably going to be nervous as it is." Judging from her current behavior, that was an understatement.

Bram scratched the nape of his neck, his expression thoughtful. "Speaking of which, we never did decide which item we're marking off the list tonight. Did you have a particular one in mind?"

Yeah. D—all of the above. Much as the idea of indulging in an all-night sexual smorgasbord fired his cylinders, he acknowledged that patience would be the name of the game this evening. Getting Lacey hot and desperate for more would ultimately buy them the opening they needed. Hopefully one taste wouldn't be enough for her, just like he knew it wouldn't be for him. "Let's play it by ear."

Bram nodded. "I'll see you at my place in a few then. Good luck with Lace."

Dragging in a deep breath, Ry watched Bram head for the kitchen. He wasn't so much worried about the heavy convincing he had ahead of him as having to fight the urge to peel off Lacey's clothes and bend her over the arm of the couch while he devoured her pussy. His cock once again nudged at his zipper, giving a resounding *hell yeah* to that scenario.

Apparently his dick hadn't gotten the memo about being patient.

Stifling a growl, he strode in the direction of Lacey's office. He was less than five feet away when her door swung open and she peeked out. His focus veered to the purse swinging from her fingertips. The little scaredy cat intended to sneak out. She turned her head and spotted him. Mouth popping into an O of surprise, she dashed toward the entrance of the restaurant. She got no more than two steps before he blocked her exit and corralled her back into her office. Ignoring her scowl, he shut the door behind him and locked it.

"What are you doing?"

"Keeping you from running and hiding."

She flung up her arms. "I was going home."

"Exactly."

"So what, I'm not allowed to leave my office now?"

"Only if you agree to have dinner with Bram and me at his house tonight."

A distinct look of panic flashed across her face. "I—I can't."

"Why?"

"I have plans."

"Yeah, with us." He stalked forward, backing Lacey into her desk. "You agreed to one item, remember?"

"I never said it'd be tonight."

"Lace, Bram and I aren't going to let you weasel your way out of this. Might as well accept it."

She reached behind her and white-knuckled the edge of her desk. "I'm not trying to get out of it."

"But you will. I know you."

A spark of angry defiance shuttled across her face. "I'm not a coward, damn it."

He crowded against her, invading her space. He could tell from the widening of her eyes and the shortening of her breath that he'd caught her off guard. He leaned down until their lips were almost touching. "Then stop acting like you are."

"Ry..."

Unable to resist the lure of kissing her a second longer, he claimed her mouth. Her lips parted on a shaky exhale and he took full advantage. Rather than thrust his way inside, he played the tip of his tongue over the edges of her teeth, teasing for deeper access. After the tiniest hesitation, her tongue met his.

Unlike their first kiss, this one was a slow, lush exploration. A promise of pleasures yet to come. He felt it, and he damn well made certain Lacey did too. Sifting his fingers through the silkiness of her shoulder-length blonde strands, he grasped her ass with his free hand. He traced the center seam of her wool slacks, a groan escaping him when he realized she was wearing a thong. He'd seen

Lacey plenty of times in a modest two-piece bathing suit that still managed to torment him and make the fit of his shorts uncomfortably snug in the groin. That was nothing compared to the torture facing him now as he imagined the soft cheeks of her ass bisected by the skimpy scrap of fabric. More than anything, he wanted to tug her pants down so he could knead and massage her butt before licking and grazing his teeth over her creamy skin. Then he'd push aside her thong and stroke his tongue from her pussy to her asshole, taking his time to properly worship every inch of her sensitive flesh.

Unfortunately, her office wasn't exactly the most private place to be at the moment, even with the door locked. Instead he made do by gripping her tighter and rubbing his denim-imprisoned erection against her belly. His mouth captured her gasp. Her hand crept around his neck, grazing his nape as her thigh shifted, sliding along his. He wasn't sure she even realized what she was doing.

It was a safe bet she had no clue what she was doing to *him*. He broke the kiss, his breath ragged. "I have half a mind to say fuck dinner and eat you instead."

Kiss-swollen lips parting, she stared at him, her pupils dilated. Her chest rose and fell on choppy, staccato inhalations.

"If you keep looking at me like that, I'm going to take it as an invitation to make good on my word. Right here, right now."

She snapped her mouth shut and pulled her hand

from him, using it to swipe a lock of her hair behind her ear. "W-what time should I be at Bram's?"

He battled the urge to grin like a fool. *Good girl.* "I was just about to drive over there. How about you ride shotgun with me?"

"But my car..."

"If you decide to head home later, I can always bring you back here."

She frowned. "Why wouldn't I be going home?"

He tried not to let his disappointment show. "I was hoping you'd be open to the possibility of spending the entire night with us."

Her eyes became shadowed with worry. "Ry..."

He stopped any forthcoming protest with a lingering brush of his lips over hers. "It's okay. If you don't feel comfortable doing that just yet, you don't have to." *But I'm damn well going to do everything I can to change your mind.*

The storm clouds in her irises cleared and she offered a tentative smile. "Thank you for understanding. You're an awesome friend."

He hugged her to him and kissed the top of her forehead. "Maybe. I know I plan on getting extra *friendly* with you before the night is done," he teased.

A rosy flush bloomed on her cheekbones. Her dusky eyelashes lowered as she stared at his chest and nibbled on her bottom lip. "Sooo...have you and Bram narrowed down which item you're helping me check off?"

"Wouldn't you like to know?"

Her gaze jerked upward, and she blinked at him. "Yeah, I would, as a matter of fact."

"Hence the reason I'm not going to tell you. Far more exciting this way."

Her eyes narrowed into slits. "I take back all the nice things I just said about you."

Chuckling, he dropped another kiss on her sulky mouth before steering her toward the door.

The butterflies dive-bombing each other in Lacey's stomach were either on a suicide mission or had just stumbled out of a kegger party. Regardless, the sensation wasn't doing much to bolster her confidence and make her feel like a vibrant sex goddess on her way to a night of kinky fun with her best buds.

Smoothing a trembling hand over her jumpy tummy, she tried to relax as Ry parked his truck and shut off the engine.

"Wait there. I don't want you slipping on your way out." Ry shoved his keys into the pocket of his leather bomber jacket before climbing from the vehicle. Pulling up his collar in defense of the cold, he hurried to her side and cracked open her door. Snowflakes clung to his glossy, midnight-black hair and his eyelashes. She couldn't resist running her fingertip over one of the thick fringes. He blinked and grinned at her. "Let me guess. I look like Frosty."

Sure, if Frosty were over six feet of hard-muscled,

sexy man candy.

He slid his hands beneath her coat and stroked the sides of her breasts, making no bones over the fact he was copping a cheap feel before he anchored his palms beneath her armpits and easily lifted her from the cab. He caught her dry look, and his wicked smile widened. The sight of it was enough to bring a surge of wetness between her legs.

Well, at least her nerves had been momentarily banished.

Ry twined his fingers with hers, and the two of them rushed toward the beckoning front porch of Bram's two-story Arts and Crafts style bungalow. As if he'd been anticipating their arrival, Bram flung open the door and she and Ry trooped into the entry, stomping their snow-covered boots on the waiting mat. Bram helped her from her coat. Like Ry, he couldn't seem to keep his hands from wandering along the outer swells of her breasts. She glanced up at him and noticed the flushed state of his face. More than likely hers was equally so, but at least she could blame it on the frigid temps outside.

Once he'd hung her coat up in the hall closet, Bram snuggled her in his arms. "I'm glad you decided to come."

"Ry didn't give me much choice," she admitted wryly.

"Hmm, remind me to thank him later."

A grunt came from Ry. "I'm standing right here. You can thank me now."

"True, but I'm kinda busy right now." Bending, Bram slid his mouth over hers. The contrast of his warm lips and breath against her colder flesh was startling. His heat managed to kindle her body in more ways than one. By the time he broke the kiss, her inner temperature had skyrocketed by at least one hundred degrees. They pulled apart and she peeked sideways. Ry was staring at them, his eyes dark and intense. There was no mistaking the obvious bulge tenting the fly of his jeans.

Wow, did watching her and Bram kissing turn him on? The notion was both odd and arousing. Ry had such a strong possessive streak. She could only guess that he tended to be just as territorial when it came to his women.

Mulling back over that last thought, she realized where her misassumption lay. She wasn't Ry's woman. Why would he care who kissed her? Furthermore, of course he'd be aroused witnessing the kiss between her and Bram. For Pete's sake, the two men intended to do a hell of a lot more than that with her together.

The reminder brought her jittery nerves back to the forefront. Despite her best efforts not to allow her mind to go there, she couldn't help wondering what exactly they had done with the female from their previous threesome experience. Obviously they'd fucked the woman, no mystery there. She'd read enough steamy ménage books to be able to figure out at least the basics of what had gone down.

If she were to be completely honest with herself, what terrified her most was the possibility of being a huge disappointment to Ry and Bram. Most likely that mystery woman had been exotic and sexy, the exact opposite of Lacey. Hell, maybe the female had been the one to proposition Bram and Ry. How could Lacey compete with that sort of brazen confidence?

Yes, it was stupid to compare herself to a faceless woman from their past, but it didn't change the fact that she was worried she'd come out lacking in retrospect. Smothering her sigh, she knelt and unzipped her boots before tugging them off. She wore thick socks, but she couldn't help being grateful for the radiant heating Bram had installed with his parquet floors. Her toes curling in appreciation of the cozy warmth, she straightened and hugged her chest.

"How about a glass of wine?" Bram offered, heading toward the kitchen. "I just opened a bottle."

A fifth of tequila was more in order, but she kept the thought to herself. She didn't want them to assume she needed to get snockered in order to go through with this. Even though she probably did.

Ry's palm rubbed her tensed back, and she looked up at him. With his free arm, he gestured toward Bram, indicating that they should follow him.

Good idea. Standing all night in the entry clearly wouldn't get them anywhere fast. Feeling like a doofus, she allowed Ry to lead her into the kitchen. While Bram grabbed a pair of crystal stemware from the rack and a cold beer from the fridge for Ry, she scooted onto one of the leather-capped barstools fronting the enormous granite-topped center island. She'd sat on this very seat numerous times, but she'd never once experienced the level of stomach-churning anxiety that she did now.

Where was the sexy Lacey from her fantasies? Figures the damn wench would abandon her in her time of need.

Bram settled her wineglass in front of her, and she picked it up to take a fortifying sip. A warm, mellow glow spread through her as the Shiraz settled in her belly. The aroma of garlic and red chilies carried from a pan sizzling on the stove. She licked her lips. "Is that Kevin's Penne Arrabiata?"

"Yep. I'm just reheating it a bit. It'll be ready in a sec."

Both Bram and Ry knew the dish was her absolute favorite. It was just one of the countless insider scoops they had on her. Knowing they'd deliberately chosen her most beloved comfort food settled her nerves and her stomach. These two men practically knew her better than she knew herself. They'd been there for her through some of the toughest times in her life. If there was anyone she trusted to embark on a sexual discovery with, it was them.

This would work. She'd make damn sure of it. Gulping another sip of wine, she silently armored her determination. Her fingers no longer displaying the trembling she'd suffered moments ago, she pushed the glass closer to the middle of the island and turned toward Ry. He smiled at her in the adorable way that always made his eyes crinkle at the corners. Leaning forward, she crushed her mouth over his, earning his harsh intake of breath. His surprise didn't last long though. Groaning, he tangled a hand in her hair, slanting her head as his tongue delved past her lips.

He kissed her like he was giving a demonstration of how he intended to make love to her—hot, deep and consuming. His other hand moved to her breast and caressed it through her clothing. A frustrated growl rumbled from him, and he reached for the hem of her sweater and tugged it upward. He broke their kiss and guided her arms over her head. She realized what he intended to do. Rather than protest, she allowed him to remove her sweater and toss it on the stool behind him.

His gaze raked her torso, lingering on the plumped cleavage peeking above the silk cups of her pink demi bra. Without saying a word, he unhooked the front closure. The weight of her breasts pushed the bra open slightly. Running his fingers beneath the straps, Ry eased them down her shoulders, forcing the garment to separate from her flesh in agonizingly slow increments. His Adam's apple bobbed, a sure sign that his lazy, tormenting movements affected him just as much as her. The edges of the silk caught on her nipples, the teasing rasp springing a moan past her lips.

Finally the fabric released her from its taunting hold, completely baring her to Ry's heated gaze. "Christ, you're fucking beautiful."

A soft scuff sounded to the left, and she turned her head to see Bram standing beside her. She'd been so ensnared in Ry's focus she hadn't heard Bram approach until then. Like Ry, he was staring at her with a dark, ravenous hunger. "He's right, Lace. Your breasts are gorgeous. Absolutely perfect."

She'd always worried they were too big, especially in the sense that they'd sag and not exactly be perky the older she got. But judging from Bram's and Ry's enamored expressions, saggy boobs were the last concern on their minds. As if to verify her assumption, Ry cupped her breast, her flesh overflowing his palm. His thumb flicked over her puckered nipple, and she gasped, a pleasurable shiver coursing along her spine. His pupils dilated, making his eyes look dark and sexy as sin. Massaging her breast, he leaned down and traced her areola with the tip of his tongue before kissing the pebbled nub. Her breath hitched and her head fell back, her eyes sliding shut. They flew open a second later when Bram's mouth closed around her other nipple.

They were both licking and sucking her breasts. *Oh God.* She'd fantasized about this very thing thousands of times yet nothing could compare to the mind-blowing reality of it. The pleasure was so intense, she worried she might pass out from it. Her fingers sifted through Ry's and Bram's hair, holding them close. Although they were equally devoted to worshipping her breasts, their style and technique came with differences. Intriguing, exciting differences that only fueled her arousal to a fever pitch. Bram's focus was strictly concentrated on her nipple, alternating between teasing flicks of his tongue and long, luscious suckling. Ry, on the other hand, occasionally licked and teased her entire breast, even using his teeth and the scruff of his days-old beard to amp up his sensual onslaught.

Just as she thought she'd go crazy from the pleasurable overload they were inflicting on her, a shrill buzzing filled the air. She jolted at the unexpected noise.

Bram released her and groaned. "Sorry. I forgot I set the timer." His expression apologetic, he abandoned her to go take care of things on the stove.

Ry's mouth reluctantly left her breast and slid along the slope of her neck before brushing over her lips. "Do you have any idea how delicious you are?"

"Even better than Kevin's Penne Arrabiata?" she couldn't help asking with a grin.

"A million times tastier." He snagged her bottom lip between his teeth and gave it a good nibble before letting her go and glancing down at her bared breasts with unabashed appreciation. "Look at you. Damn, you should be topless all the time."

She rolled her eyes. "Yeah, that'd go over great at work." Leaning past him, she attempted to grab her sweater, but Ry used his foot to kick the stool out of her reach. She frowned. "I need that."

"Why?"

She shoved her arms over her chest. "I am *not* going to eat with my boobs hanging out like this, Ryan Hollister."

A chuckle came from Bram. "Ooh, she called you by your full name. You're in trouble now, bud."

Ry didn't look the least bit worried. "I'm only trying to

save her from slopping on her sweater. You'd think she'd appreciate my ingenuity."

"Puh-lease. We all know who's the messier eater here." She offered Ry a pointed stare.

"Can I help it if I enjoy savoring my meals?" His smile was slow and sexy, leaving her with little doubt that he was imagining her as his next main course. "Still, no one is going to accuse me of not playing fair." He hefted from his seat and tugged his ribbed Henley over his head. His biceps flexing, he dropped the garment on top of her sweater.

A herd of rhinos could have trooped through the kitchen and it wouldn't have distracted her from ogling Ry's sculpted pecs and six pack. She didn't know many men who possessed bodies capable of making a woman orgasm just by staring at them. Somehow she had the great fortune to be within breathing distance of *two* such individuals.

The overhead track lighting cast a golden glow across Ry's chest, beckoning her. Giving in to the urge that'd tormented her for as long as she could remember, she hopped to her feet and ran her fingertips along his torso. A moan tumbled from him. She imagined that same sound tearing from him while he rode her hard, his balls slapping against her wet flesh. Her clit throbbed. Her hands venturing along his abdomen, she ducked her head and sucked the flat nub of his nipple into her mouth.

"*Jesus.*" Ry's warm, velvety skin quivered beneath her

touch, filling her with a wanton glee over affecting him like this. It was a heady realization.

The clatter of plates close by announced that Bram had rejoined them. "Damn. When's my turn?"

She stopped licking and sucking Ry for a moment and glanced at Bram. "You still have your shirt on."

"Hell, not for long." Reaching behind him with one hand, Bram yanked his crewneck off in one fell swoop. She would have laughed, but the sight of his outrageously gorgeous chest turned her mouth dry as sand. Crooking one finger, she invited him closer. She scooted aside and directed Bram to stand next to Ry. With the two men shoulder to shoulder, there was no denying the pure, masculine beauty of their hard, fit bodies.

I must have earned mega karma points somewhere to deserve this bounty. Barely caging her hungry groan, she smoothed her palms across both of their broad chests before swirling her tongue over Bram's nipple. His breath caught in his throat. Just as she'd discovered with their oral techniques, Bram and Ry also came with uniquely different tastes. While Ry was all forest and musk, Bram's skin held a slight citrusy tang, as if he consisted of the sun itself. They were both scrumptious beyond words.

She alternated her licks and nibbles between them, making sure neither was shortchanged. At some point their hands returned to her breasts, massaging and caressing her until she was gasping and leaning on them for support. Someone's palm cupped her between her legs and she trembled. The teasing pressure of the fingers riding against her pussy tantalized, but they weren't nearly enough. Particularly with two layers of fabric separating her from their touch.

As if he intuited her frustration, Ry pressed a hot, open-mouthed kiss along her temple. He stroked her cheek, his mouth moving toward her ear. "Show us how to please you, baby."

"Y-you are."

"No. Not enough." Ry removed his hand from her pussy and worked her zipper down before hunkering in front of her. He eased her slacks past her hips and coaxed her to step out of them when they pooled around her ankles. His mouth nuzzled her tummy before he circled the outer rim of her bellybutton with his tongue.

She squirmed and dug her fingers into his thick, soft hair. "Please."

He looked up at her. "Please what?"

"I don't know. *Anything.* Just kiss and lick me."

"You can do better than that, Lace. Give me specifics."

Her skin flushed at his words and the heat in his eyes. It was crazy how much her fantasy version of Ry matched up with the real man. "I—I don't know if I can."

"Yes, you do." He glanced at Bram. Once again, some form of unspoken communication must have passed between them because Bram cleared the pair of nearby stools away from the island and pushed the plates of pasta out of reach. She wasn't certain why he did that, until Ry lifted her into his arms and settled her onto the counter.

His thumbs tucked into the elastic of her thong and dragged it down her legs. Her butt absorbed the granite's chill, but she barely registered it as Ry and Bram stared at her glistening folds. Ry's fist tightened on her thong, his jaw tense. She shifted her attention to Bram and snagged his gaze. He licked his lips, and she inched her thighs wider apart, hoping to tempt him into action.

A husky chuckle came from Ry. "Nice try, baby. But you're not getting out of this that easy."

She blinked at him. "Get out of what?"

"Checking off item number two."

It took a moment to remember her reason for being there. The list. She racked her brain, trying to recall what number two entailed.

"You're gonna play with your sweet pussy for us, Lace," Bram said, apparently taking pity on her memory lapse.

"What?" She slashed her gaze between the two of them. "But...I thought you wanted to do it for me."

"Believe me, we will. But first you're going to show us exactly how you like to be touched. How you make yourself come." Almost as if he were unconscious of what he was doing, Ry bunched her thong in his fist and pressed the silk to his nose. His eyes closed as a rapturous groan rumbled from his chest.

She stared at him, her heart missing a beat. Okay, how the hell had she guessed *that* right?

Ry opened his eyes again, revealing the fierce fire kindled within their depths. "This is your chance to teach us how to please you. Trust me, this is a good thing."

She bit her lip and let his words sink in. What he was suggesting actually made a lot of sense, and truthfully, she was grateful that he and Bram cared about ensuring her pleasure. She didn't have much previous experience with men who weren't looking for a fast way to get *their* rocks off. It made her want to discover all the ways that she could please Ry and Bram too. "I'll do it. But only if you show me how *you* like to be touched."

Quiet laughter fell from Ry and Bram. They glanced at each other before offering her matching grins.

"What?" she demanded.

"Darlin', you don't hafta worry about that," Bram said with a shake of his head. "Our anatomy isn't quite as complex as yours. You'll probably only have to look at our dicks to make them blow."

She wasn't ready to take them entirely on their word. "Strip. Now."

More chuckles came from the guys. "Damn, Lace. Where'd this bossy side of you come from?" Bram thumbed the top button open on his jeans and rasped his zipper down. His smile stretched wide, giving her a nice flash of his teeth. "I like it."

She planted her palms on the counter and leaned back as Bram and Ry kicked free of their jeans. Mouthwatering as their strong, muscular calves and thighs were, it was the startlingly huge erections snugged within their white briefs that held her rapt attention. Her hand trailed between her legs and her fingertips skimmed through her slick wetness. She didn't even realize what she was doing until Ry's and Bram's groans broke through her concentration. She jerked her focus upward and noticed their unblinking gazes were glued to the motions of her fingers. Her hand halted.

"Don't stop," Ry admonished, his voice strained.

She cupped her mound protectively. "Please. I don't want to be the only one doing this."

Ry and Bram automatically reached for their briefs and peeled them off. Their cocks sprang free—long, thick and unbelievably hard. Her clit pulsed without her even rubbing it, and moisture pooled between her legs. More than anything, she wanted to feel the silky-steel length of their shafts gliding in her palms. Or better yet, sliding along the wet folds of her labia before sinking deep inside her. Just the thought of it sent a sharp, needy ache through her core, and she whimpered.

Ry circled his cock with his fist and gave it a lazy, indulgent stroke. Bram, on the other hand, pumped his with a firmer grip, making his abs quiver and the veins in his forearm stand out in stark relief. She watched them both, yet again fascinated by the marked differences in their techniques.

"Baby, I think you're neglecting something." Ry nodded toward the motionless fingers resting between her legs.

Okay, she could definitely do this. Not like there wasn't plenty of wicked inspiration standing right in front of her. Letting her thighs fall open a bit more, she glossed her fingertips over her soaked slit, moving toward her clit. When she came in contact with the throbbing nubbin, she shivered and arched her back.

"*Fuck.*" A hoarse groan ripped from Bram, and he squeezed the base of his cock so hard his knuckles whitened.

Ry paid him no mind and instead continued to stare at her. He worked his fist along the rigid length of his shaft, curling his palm slightly as he rubbed over the rosy, plum-shaped cap, spreading a drop of precome with his thumb. "Is stroking your clit enough to get you off?"

A warning pulse trembled through her at his question. She struggled to hold it off, to not succumb to the looming orgasm. "Sometimes," she gasped, her gaze latched to his thick erection. God, she wanted him inside her. So badly, she shook from the desperate need of it. "But I...I want—" She tried to get the words out, but the sensations building inside her could no longer be ignored. "*Oooh.*" She clamped her legs together, but that only intensified the pressure on her clit.

The orgasm slammed into her, making her shudder and gasp. She was acutely aware of Ry's and Bram's hot gazes cataloging every detail of her climax the entire time the quakes rolled through her body. A distant part of her wondered why she didn't feel embarrassed. Moments after the glow began to settle, Ry's arms tucked beneath her legs and he scooped her against his chest. She snuggled into him, too limp and content to do much else. He carried her down the hall and into Bram's bedroom.

She giggled as the three of them climbed into the massive California King bed. "Something tells me we're not going to be eating for a while."

Ry scooted between her thighs, bracing them with his wide shoulders. His expression was pure sin. "Speak for yourself." Beard scruff tickled her sensitive flesh as his mouth closed around her pussy. He sucked on the folds of her labia, using the tip of his tongue to tease her clit.

She jerked, the sensations almost too much to take. Ry held her hips firm to the mattress, giving her no option but to submit to his exquisite torment. Bram leaned over her and suckled her breasts, each devastating tug on her nipples resulting in an echoing pulse through her clit. Ry's mouth left her pussy.

She wanted to weep at the cruel abandonment, until Bram stretched across her and coasted his tongue along her slit. "Fuck, you taste amazing."

Ry rumbled his agreement before sinking two fingers inside her. "You're so tight and wet. Let me feel you come again, baby."

Together he and Bram brought her to a dazzling peak. She hovered there, suspended for a long moment before her body shattered. She cried out, her pussy clenching, milking Ry's fingers with strong spasms.

Bram sat back on his haunches, his expression pained as he squeezed his cock. She stared at his gorgeous, straining shaft and licked her lips. Gaze riveted on her prize, she inched closer and kissed the swollen head. His salty, musky essence quickly became addictive, and she pulled his hand away so she could take more of him into her mouth. His groans filled her ears, encouraging her to suck him deeper. "Jesus, Lace. That's fucking good."

The mattress dipped, and she looked over to see Ry rummaging in the nightstand.

"Other drawer," Bram said, his breath a harsh rasp.

Ry returned to the bed and tossed a handful of condoms onto the comforter. Her pulse sped up at the implications of needing that many condoms, but a moment later, when Ry sheathed himself and positioned his cock at her slick entrance, the only thought consuming her was the anticipation of finally having him buried inside her. He nudged past her opening, stretching her. She undulated her hips, desperately attempting to lodge him deeper. He tightened his grip on her, refusing to accommodate. "We're going to test your multitasking skills. The idea is to have all of us come together. You up for it?"

An agonized sound came from Bram as he leaned over her. "I'm seconds away from blowing."

"Tough. Count baseball stats or something." With tormenting laziness, Ry thrust into her. His gliding penetration was so slow she felt the luscious friction of every vein in his cock through the condom. At the tail end of his stroke, he flexed his hips with a slight twist, rubbing her clit with his pubic bone. She gasped around Bram, earning another of his tortured grunts.

"Goddamn it, I'm gonna come," Bram bit out between harsh, ragged pants.

"No you're not. You can take it." Ry stroked in and out of her, his rhythm steady. "Imagine if you were where I am, balls-deep in tight, wet, luscious pussy."

"You are one sadistic son of a bitch." The words sounded like they'd been ground between Bram's teeth.

A smoky laugh fell from Ry. It caressed her, making her shiver and writhe on his cock. Ry's motions faltered for a moment before he suddenly pumped into her harder. Deeper. Gripping her hips, he pulled her into his thrusts. "God, I want to feel you come around me."

She gave a delirious moan, and Ry strummed her clit. "Keep sucking his cock, baby. Use your mouth and your pussy to make us come with you."

His soft command was all the invitation she needed. Angling her head back, she swallowed Bram down her throat and squeezed her vaginal muscles. The groan that shook from Ry verified that all those Kegel exercises really paid off. Breathing through her nose, she continued to suck and swallow Bram's cock. His balls tightened and his thighs were rock hard, hinting how close he was. Ry pounded into her now, his determination to send her over the edge creating a lush spiral of pleasure within her.

Her entire existence narrowed to the cocks filling her mouth and pussy.

The orgasm started in her toes, rapidly spreading upward and outward in an unending tremble through her body. Tears streamed from her eyes, as much from the emotional tide crashing over her as the overwhelming pleasure of the climax. The masculine groans surrounding her were her first clues that Ry and Bram were making good on the promise of simultaneous orgasms. Through her sensual fog she realized Bram's come was spurting down her throat while Ry's cock throbbed inside her. It was enough to trigger another wave of orgasm, and she moaned around Bram's pulsing shaft.

Nothing should feel this good. Be this incredible.

Even as she began to lose consciousness, a resounding truth clanged through her mind.

No fantasy could ever compare to this.

CHAPTER SEVEN

Bram awoke before Ry or Lacey. He used it to his full advantage, taking the opportunity to look his fill of the woman who'd consumed his thoughts and dreams for the past fifteen years.

Jesus, she was everything he'd ever wanted, wrapped up in a sweet, sexy package that made his heart sing and his cock stiff. Reaching down, he tamed his morning erection with a light squeeze. Unfortunately, touching his dick only brought to mind the mind-blowing pleasure of Lacey deep-throating him last night. He didn't think he'd ever come so hard or long before in his life. Watching Ry fucking her, his cock drenched from her pussy, had only made the experience a million times more amazing.

He'd always suspected it would be this way. If he were being honest with himself, it was probably a large part of the reason why he'd encouraged Ry with that one-time threesome all those years ago. In the back of his mind, he'd wanted it to be Lacey squirming and gasping and coming between them.

Last night only proved he'd been right to want it. The three of them were meant for this. Maybe Lacey didn't fully see it, or Ry. But it was true. They fulfilled something in each other, brought a dynamic to the relationship that wouldn't exist outside of the threesome. Yeah, he had no problem making love to Lacey without Ry in the room, but the fact his best friend was right there too...talk about unbelievably hot. He fucking loved getting to see Ry take control, directing everyone's pleasure. It freed Bram to immerse himself in the moment, to let his inner sexual beast howl and fuck to his heart's content.

His cock bobbed against his stomach, making it clear that it was in the mood for a little lovin'. His gaze raked Lacey's smooth, creamy skin and settled on the patch of pale blonde curls at the apex of her thighs. He knew precisely how he wanted to wake her up. Salivating in anticipation, he scooted closer to the foot of the bed and slid his hand over her mound. She murmured in her sleep but didn't immediately awaken. Using his thumb to ease back the tiny protective hood of her clit, he brushed the nub with a soft kiss before toggling it with feather-light licks. She wiggled, her sensitive tissues quickly becoming wetter and wetter with each persuasive lap of his tongue. He sensed the tension building in her body and glanced up to find her sleepy eyes locked on him. Hers weren't the only ones.

Ry rolled onto his elbow, presumably to get a better look. Like Bram, his cock was definitely sporting some morning wood. "How does she taste?"

"Fucking awesome."

Lacey shuddered, perhaps in response to the humming vibration of his words against her pussy. Ry cupped her breast, massaging it lightly before rolling her nipple between his thumb and forefinger. "Does Bram's mouth feel good on you, baby?"

She gave an exuberant nod, and Ry chuckled. "What do you like best? Having your clit licked or sucked?"

"B-both." She gave a breathless murmur when Ry leaned down to kiss her. Bram could see their tongues gliding together. The fact that he was going down on Lacey at the same time only made the whole scene even more erotic. Lifting her hips a fraction, he sucked on her clit before sliding his tongue inside her. He drew on every ounce of oral skill he possessed while he ate her out, his excitement rising—along with his cock—with each broken gasp and moan that escaped Lacey. Suddenly her body tensed and her hips gave an involuntary jerk. Ry's mouth cut off her keening cry while her clit beat beneath Bram's tongue. He continued lapping at her until she slumped into the bedding. His cock was so hard and dripping enough precome that it'd left a wet spot on the comforter.

Ry—being the excellent wingman he was—snagged one of the condoms and tossed it to Bram. "Suit up."

Hell, he didn't need to be told twice. He ripped the foil packet open with his teeth and made short work of sheathing his cock. He started to position himself between Lacey's legs, but Ry shook his head and pointed to the empty spot beside her. His brain giving way to the sexual beast panting inside him, Bram rolled onto his back and reached for Lacey. With Ry's help, he eased her onto his lap so that she was straddling him. He nudged into her slit, and she slowly sank onto him, her pussy hugging him in a warm, snug embrace.

Fuck. He had no idea how Ry managed to hold off from immediately blowing the second he thrust into Lacey last night. The guy must have restraint more powerful than fucking Kryptonite. Gritting his teeth, Bram flexed his fingers on Lacey's thighs, trying to concentrate on anything other than the tiny aftershocks rippling through the wet, silky flesh surrounding him as Lacey started to come down from her earlier orgasm. The lure to give in to the fierce urge tightening his balls was irresistible, but he wanted to show that he had just as much control as Ry. Plus he wanted to make Lacey come again. Maybe if they kept her showered in orgasms, she'd be more willing to make this threesome a permanent aspect.

Ry moved behind Lacey, supporting her with one arm banded around her waist. He did something with his other hand that caused Lacey's eyes to widen and lose their glassy, sensual haze. She swallowed. "Okay, I know I had anal on the list, but seven a.m. on a workday morning is a little too soon for that."

A chuckle floated from Ry. "Relax, that's not my intention."

"Then why is your cock—" Lacey broke off on a shaky groan. "Oh God, that feels good."

Bram had no idea what exactly Ry was doing but judging from the way Lacey shuddered and arched her back she was loving the hell out of it. Watching her reaction was enough to make Bram's cock swell even more. A moment later, the head of Ry's cock bumped into Bram's ball sac. He jolted slightly at the contact. Shit. Well that explained what Ry had been up to—sliding his dick along the crack of Lacey's ass.

"Sorry," Ry offered with a wry grin. "That was an accident."

Bram cleared his throat. "No problem. Just don't let that thing slip and go in the wrong hole. I love you, man, but not *that* much." He tuned out Ry's laugh as Lacey gaped at him.

"Y-you can feel him...down there?" Another shiver coursed through her, and she closed her eyes on a soft moan.

"Does the idea of that turn you on?" Ry's expression held one hundred degrees of wickedness as he nipped Lacey's earlobe. "Dirty girl."

She shifted her head to the side and met Ry's lips. Bram watched them engage in a hot, open-mouthed kiss that hardened his cock until he thought it would explode. Unable to remain still a second longer, he pumped his hips, surging deeper inside her. She groaned into Ry's mouth before looking down at Bram. "You feel...incredible."

"So do you, Lace." He offered her a strained smile. "In fact, I'm having a hard time not shooting too soon. No pun intended."

"You need to come?" She snagged her bottom lip between her teeth and rocked on top of him in a way that made his eyes cross.

He quickly caught her around the waist, stalling her. "Not before you, darlin'."

"I already did. It might take a while to get there again."

Not if he had anything to say about it. He shot a look toward Ry and noticed the determined gleam in his best friend's gaze. Good. They were of similar minds.

Ry pulled Lacey flush against his chest, and her resulting gasp hinted that her ass cheeks were pillowed around his dick. With both of his hands now freed, Ry cupped Lacey's breasts, massaging them in rhythm to Bram's thrusts. Her pussy clenched around Bram, a sign that she was drawing closer to the peak.

He trailed his palm down to where they were joined and ghosted his thumb over her clit. The slippery nubbin enticed him into tasting her once more, and he pulled his hand away just long enough to suck her essence from his finger. Lacey stared at him as if mesmerized, and he grinned at her. "Can you blame me? You're too delicious to resist."

Ry nuzzled her neck. "Baby, don't let him hog all that

honey. Give me some too."

She seemed at a loss for what to do so Bram guided her fingers down to her clit. A pretty shade of pink bloomed across her face as she comprehended the meaning behind Ry's request. Bram found it adorable that she could still blush after everything the three of them had done together.

Ry grasped her hand and lifted it to his lips. As he sucked her fingers into his mouth, a strong spasm trembled through Lacey and she cried out. Her pussy clamped hard around Bram's cock, making his breath hiss between his teeth. He managed one pistoning stroke before his balls unloaded, jetting what felt like endless amounts of come into the condom. His eyes rolled back, his body shaking. The moan that tore from his throat sounded like it came from a different man—one who was having his life force sucked from him.

Hell, he probably was.

It felt like an eternity passed before he gathered enough strength to refocus on Lacey and Ry. From the look of it, she'd only just started to recover herself. Ry continued caressing her through the ebbing tide of her orgasm. When she slumped forward, Ry eased her off Bram and onto her back. Mindful of his full condom, Bram weakly swung his legs over the side of the mattress and staggered into the bathroom. After disposing of the condom, he splashed his face with cold water, the briskness of it snapping him back to his senses.

Holy fuck. He'd never experienced anything remotely

like that before in his life. Every prior sexual encounter that didn't include Lacey and Ry was suddenly insignificant. And it wasn't merely about the sex. Though God knows, it was fucking incredible. Nothing could touch the love that he felt for those two people out there.

Maybe it wouldn't make sense to most that he could love Ry like a brother and not be jealous about sharing Lacey with him. The dynamics of this relationship would certainly be frowned upon by the majority of folks he knew. Probably the only one who wouldn't be freaked out by it was Jana. But then again, his little sis was likely into even more kink than he was, judging from the paraphernalia she carried in her shop. Not that he wanted to have his suspicions confirmed. Some things he was happier remaining in blissful ignorance of.

Running his damp fingers through his hair to tame it into submission, he strode back out into the bedroom. Ry was stretched between Lacey's spread thighs, his tensed glutes flexing as he fucked her with a deceptively lazy rhythm. It might have been slow as molasses on a winter morning, but apparently it was getting to Lacey enough that her fingernails were digging into Ry's flanks.

And truthfully, it was getting to Bram too. Despite his having just come his brains out, his cock thickened with renewed life. Stroking his growing erection, he stepped closer to the bed. If Ry was aware that he and Lacey had a captive audience, he didn't let on, and instead just kept pumping away while his mouth played with her nipples.

Lacey, on the other hand, caught Bram's stare. She swallowed, her breath audibly hitching in her throat. He had the feeling she was as aroused by him watching her as he was.

Desperately wanting to see more, he moved toward the foot of the bed. This angle gave him a clear view of Ry's cock tunneling in and out of Lacey's incredibly wet pussy.

"I wish I could spend all morning buried inside you. Feeling you come." Ry's voice was the consistency of gravel. "Come on my cock, baby. Fuck yeah, like that. So good."

The slick sounds of them fucking, as well as the sight of Lacey's soft, pink flesh clinging so tightly to Ry's glistening shaft, ripped a thunderbolt of lust and desire through Bram. With no warning, his cock fired off again. There wasn't as much to discharge this time, considering how hard he came minutes earlier, but it still blew his mind that it happened without him even touching his dick. Through his climax-induced brain fog, he heard Ry's broken groan as he also came.

Thank Christ. Because if Bram had been inclined to listen to or watch one more second of their lovemaking, there was a good chance he would have come another time or two dozen. Which might have very well killed him.

But, *damn*, what a way to go.

CHAPTER EIGHT

If she'd thought she'd been obsessed with sexual fantasies starring her best friends before, it was nothing compared to the torture she was going through now.

Lacey took a deep, steadying breath as Ry and Bram leaned against the metal prep table in the kitchen while the head chef, Kevin, droned on about the menu specials he wanted to include for Friday night's Beach Party. She caught the occasional mention of coconut shrimp and Caribbean jerk chicken kabobs, but honestly, Kevin might as well be asking for PB&J sandwiches for all the attention she was paying to his requests. All she could think about was having Bram and Ry inside her again. Sooner rather than later.

God, how could she still be so wet and desperate for sex after all of the orgasms she'd shuddered through last night and this morning? She was turning into a damn nympho, for Pete's sake. And the two mouthwateringly gorgeous men across from her were totally to blame.

As if they'd somehow tuned in to her irritable brainwaves, Ry and Bram glanced her way. To the casual observer, their smiles were completely innocent. But Lacey knew better. Beneath their innocuous façade she heard their silent transmission loud and clear. It basically translated to, *"Later it's your pussy and our cocks. Get ready to scream your head off."*

She hunched her shoulders, praying that the position puffed out her blouse enough to hide the perkiness of her nipples. Damn it, why hadn't she kept her suit jacket on? Of course, she should probably be grateful that Ry generously stopped by her house before heading here this morning so that she could change. Otherwise it might have been a little difficult—and embarrassing—explaining to the curious staff members why she was wearing the same clothes she'd left in last night.

Once Kevin was finished with his presentation and the go ahead was given for the menu, she snuck from the kitchen and escaped into her office for some much-needed space from the sexy signals Ry and Bram exuded. Much as she loved them *and* all their mental foreplay, they were playing havoc with her sanity and concentration.

Shoving a wisp of hair away from her perspiring forehead, she fanned her overheated face and reached for the catalog of chef supplies resting on the corner of her desk. She managed to leaf through a couple pages before her office door opened and the two men intent on driving her insane with lust trooped into her office. She gave them a wary look as her nipples tightened. It was insane the power they had over her body.

Ry eased the door shut and offered a devilish grin. "What's the matter? You look all flushed."

"Yeah, kinda hot and bothered," Bram added with a sexy chuckle that made her pussy flood with moisture.

Rotten bastards. She flipped the catalog shut and tried her best to appear unaffected and unaroused. "It's warm in here. No doubt that's why our heating bills have been through the roof lately."

Amusement etched Ry's features. "So what do you suggest we do? Crank the thermostat down to fifty degrees and let the customers turn into walking popsicles?"

"No, smartass."

Ry abandoned the doorway and strode to her desk. He turned her chair so that she was facing him and leaned down, boxing her in with his outstretched arms. The smolder in his eyes was enough to add an extra layer of sweat onto her skin. "I got the impression this morning that you like my ass just fine. Even have the indents from your nails to prove it."

Her mind immediately tracked to the scene in question, when he'd been fucking her slow and deep, teasing her with his thick, hard cock while Bram watched, enthralled. She wiggled in her seat, biting back a moan at the sweet and agonizing friction of her panties rubbing along her slit. She returned Ry's stare for as long as she could handle before the intensity swirling between them became too much to take. Glancing sideways, she became ensnared in Bram's equally entrancing gaze. The ramifications of the naughty acts the three of them had indulged in slammed into her, leaving her feeling vulnerable and oddly shy.

Ry and Bram had witnessed a side of her that until last night hadn't existed outside of her fantasies. They could profess all they wanted that none of this would affect their friendship, but the reality was that it already had. Their trio had crossed a line that there was no returning from.

"Lace?" Ry's knuckles brushed her cheek, drawing her focus back to him. Clouds of worry shadowed his eyes. "Is everything okay?"

She bit her lip and nodded—perhaps a little too fast, since Ry didn't exactly look convinced. Bram joined them, his expression equally concerned. "You're not regretting sleeping with us, are you?"

Leave it to Bram to read her mind and get to the point in the bluntest way possible.

"No, of course not." Her cheeks heated again, and she laughed softly. "You both have given me more orgasms than I thought were humanly possible. I'd be an idiot to regret that."

Ry's fingers grazed the underside of her jaw. "We want to give you a lot more. Are you up for it?"

Although she'd been expecting them to, they hadn't pressed her last night or this morning about marking off any more items on her list. It looked like it was now time to commit to it fully. And did it really make much difference? She'd already stepped into the fire. It was too late to worry about getting burned. She sucked in a steadying breath and released it. "Yes, but this time I get to choose."

There was no mistaking the relief that swept over Ry's and Bram's features. Ry—being the one most advantageously positioned—kissed her first, his tongue thrusting deep. By the time he pulled back, she'd melted into a mindless puddle of goo. She barely had the chance to regain her breath or composure before Bram took up where Ry left off, his devouring kiss officially killing the few remaining brain cells she had left. His mouth retreated and she slumped into her chair, boneless. And hornier than she'd been five minutes ago.

Ry grinned at her. "So, what sexiness are we getting up to tonight?"

She wasn't too brain fried to recognize a golden opportunity for payback. Cocking an eyebrow, she offered them a gloating smile. "Wouldn't you like to know?"

The next five hours flew by in a productive blur. Somehow Lacey calmed her raging libido *and* got last night's receipts logged into the spreadsheet in addition to locating a new produce supplier. She even managed to get some online Christmas shopping done. Logging off her computer, she gave herself a mental high-five. "Yeah, go me."

Her office door swung open, allowing in some of the bar noise as well as Jana Colton. Lacey couldn't help laughing as she took in Jana's outfit. The tight black leather skirt and form-fitting cashmere sweater were standard fare, but the red-and-green-striped tights and Santa hat were obviously a nod to the season. "You look like a dominatrix elf."

Jana pretended to crack a whip through the air. "Someone's gotta keep those pointy-eared bastards in line."

"You do realize that remark will probably earn you a lump of coal in your stocking this year, right?"

A wicked grin curled Jana's mouth. "Says the girl with the *Naughty List.*"

Lacey groaned. "You're never going to let me live that down, are you?"

Jana sashayed to the desk and plopped her butt onto the nearest corner. "Can you blame me? You don't spring kinky sex on a gal and not expect a reaction."

"Sorry, that whole fiasco was a mistake. You weren't supposed to have actually gotten that email. Neither were Ry and Bram."

Jana's artfully shaded eyes widened and a chortling laugh sprang free. "Hoo boy. That must have triggered one hell of an interesting conversation."

Lacey averted her gaze and fiddled with her computer keys. A long, awkward silence stretched between them until she couldn't take it anymore, and she looked up to find Jana gaping at her.

"You totally had sex with them, didn't you?" Just like with Bram, subtlety wasn't exactly Jana's strong suit.

"Uh..."

"Oh my God. You *did.*" Jana hopped down from the desk and plunked her hands on her hips, her expression accusing. "Were you intending to keep this juicy secret all to yourself?"

"Yeah, pretty much."

Jana didn't appear mollified by the admission. "Why?"

"Hello. One of the men in question is your brother. Kind of weird."

"Good point." Giving a twitch of her nose, Jana returned to her previous perch. "But as long as you keep the details about Bram to a minimum, I still want to hear the whole dirty scoop." Jana's eyes twinkled with conspiratorial glee. "Okay, I've gotta ask it. Does Ry have a huge cock? Because I swear to God, it looks like he's packing a bratwurst down there. Or maybe a chub of bologna."

As familiar as she was with Jana's typical train of thought, Lacey still choked on a cough. "I can't believe you just compared a dick to packaged meat."

Jana's smile was less than angelic. "Can I help it that I like my meat metaphors?"

Lacey opened her mouth to comment just as her cell phone shrilled the opening bars of the *I Love Lucy* theme song—the ringtone for Lacey's mom. She shot Jana an apologetic glance. "Sorry, I've got to get this." Clicking the

Talk button, she snugged the phone between her ear and shoulder while she dumped her purse onto the top of her desk. "Hey, Mom. Did you and Dad get the package I sent down there yet?"

A snicker came from Jana. "You said package."

Ignoring her friend's adolescent humor, Lacey listened to her mom's assurance that FedEx had indeed delivered the box of presents, as well as Lucy McGuire's insistence that not one of them would be opened until Lacey flew down to join them for a post-holiday celebration after the new year. Lacey's parents were just one of the many snowbirds who abandoned Michigan at the first sign of snow, not to return until the temps became hospitable again in late spring. Much as Lacey missed not getting to spend Christmas with them, this time of the season was too hectic to take off to Florida for even a couple of days, much less a week.

The phone conversation shifted gears slightly as Lacey's mom inquired how everything was going at the Dockside. When asked how Ry and Bram were doing, Lacey blushed. She'd known the question was coming since her mom adored both men and tended to treat them as her surrogate sons, but Lacey couldn't help worrying that some hidden tone in her voice would give away the fact that she was involved in a kinky threesome with Ry and Bram.

Sheesh. Paranoid much? "Um, they're good. Everyone's good." *Oh God, I'm repeating myself. Like that's not suspicious at all.* "What did they get me for

Christmas?" *The best sex ever.* Her cheeks combusting, she slashed her gaze toward Jana and noticed the younger woman's smirk. "I don't know, Mom. They're keeping it a surprise until the big day. Listen, I hate to cut this short, but I was about to head out. How about I give you a call later tonight so we can chat longer? Great, it's a plan. Love to you and Dad too." She jabbed the disconnect button and groaned. "Please tell me I sounded halfway normal during that conversation."

"Yep, you handled it like a pro." Jana cocked her head to the side, her expression thoughtful. "So I take it your folks didn't get your accidental email?"

"No, thank God." Lacey scrubbed her hands over her face. "I never thought I'd actually be grateful for my parents' stubborn decision not to join the twenty-first century and get a computer."

Jana's scrutiny continued to bore into Lacey. She wiggled in her seat, feeling uncomfortably like a bug under a microscope. "Why are you looking at me like that?"

"I'm just wondering if you have any intention of telling anyone about what's going on with you, Ry and Bram."

She gaped at Jana. "What am I supposed to do? Announce to my mom and dad that I'm sleeping with two men? Gee, *that'd* make a great Hallmark moment."

"I don't just mean your folks. What about the rest of your friends? The people here." Jana waved an arm toward the doorway.

"It's nobody's business. Besides, it's only a little sexual fling. There's no need to make a big deal out of it."

Jana kept giving her that shrewd, probing look that was more penetrating than an X-ray machine. "Are you sure about that?"

"Yes. Why wouldn't I be?"

"Because you're not the kind of woman who indulges in casual, kinky affairs."

Out of nowhere, Olivia Barnam's scornful words from the other day raced inside Lacey's head. *"You're boring. A goody-goody who doesn't know the first thing about how to please a man."* An icy chill crept over her, followed by crushing uncertainty. Struggling to pry free of the negativity threatening to hold her hostage, she glared at Jana. "Well clearly you're wrong, because that's precisely what I'm doing."

"I'm not trying to pick a fight with you." Lines of worry bracketed Jana's forehead. "It's just that after everything that happened with Dan...I don't want to see you get hurt again."

"I won't." She'd learned her lesson about opening her heart to that kind of pain. It wouldn't happen again. No damn way.

CHAPTER NINE

"Are you sure you're ready for this?" Ry took his eyes off the road long enough to glance toward the passenger seat, where Lacey sat huddled in her oversized down coat.

"It's on my list, isn't it?"

The backseat creaked as Bram leaned toward the console. "Yeah, but we sort of assumed you'd want to gradually work up toward going to the sex club."

Lacey's chin adopted a stubborn slant. "No, I want to do it now. I'm fully capable of handling it."

Ry returned his focus to driving, but he continued to mull Lacey's behavior. She'd been edgy from the moment he and Bram picked her up at her house. Maybe she was nervous about the upcoming night. If that was the case, he didn't know why she insisted on doing the sex club so soon. Still, he knew better than to argue with her when she was in this kind of a mood. Better to go along with her wishes and soothe her back into the uninhibited, sensual frame of mind she'd been in earlier this morning.

The reminder of the sexy adventures the three of them got up to in Bram's bed only served to make Ry's cock painfully hard behind his fly. He never would have imagined that sharing Lacey with his best friend would be something he'd be okay with, much less enjoy.

Enjoy? Hell, who was he kidding? He fucking loved every second of it. Sure, at first a spark of jealousy ignited in him when he'd watched Bram kissing Lacey in the entryway of the house. But for some odd reason, the moment all of their clothes came off, everything changed. Bram had ceased to be a threat, or competition, and instead became an ally in making Lacey's wickedest fantasies come true. Plus there was no denying that Ry got off on being in charge. Maybe it had something to do with the fact he'd had so little control over his life while growing up and now he hungered for that aspect. Who knows? The only thing he could say with any certainty was that he'd gotten a taste of how things could be for the three of them. There was no way he'd settle for less.

The exit he needed popped into view, and he maneuvered into the far lane. Seconds later, he took the off-ramp and drove into the city limits. Traffic was light, cutting the drive time significantly. Less than fifteen minutes later, he pulled into the relatively empty parking lot of Club Arabesque. The small amount of cars didn't necessarily mean anything. There were plenty of club patrons who preferred a low profile and parked their vehicles in one of the lots farther down the street and hoofed it over on foot. Still, he hoped for Lacey's sake that some of the club's more interesting characters were too busy with holiday festivities to make an appearance tonight. She might profess to be ready for this, but he wasn't entirely convinced.

Leaving the toasty warmth of the truck behind, the three of them approached the gothic, multistory stone building. Not for the first time, he couldn't help thinking how ironic and twisted it was that a former church now housed an underground sex club. He glanced at Lacey and noticed that her teeth were chattering. Either the cold was getting to her or her nerves were kicking in. Dropping an arm around her shoulders, he hugged her close. He met Bram's gaze over the top of her head and a shared look passed between them, a nonverbal pact that together they'd do everything in their power to make this a positive experience for Lacey.

At the door, a burly bouncer who probably bench-pressed refrigerators for the shit of it asked for ID. Once the man ascertained that Bram was a paying member of the club, he stepped aside and allowed them admittance. The interior of the building offered a warm reprieve from the frigid temps outside—something that the majority of scantily clad patrons no doubt appreciated. Apparently also feeling the effects of the central heating, Lacey shrugged from her coat and draped it over her arm.

A woman dressed in a red latex corset that exposed her breasts—pierced nipples and all—strutted past them leading a shirtless young man by a studded collar and leash. Ry checked Lacey for her reaction and wasn't disappointed as her mouth fell open. This night would be a revelation for her in more ways than one. As if they were of one mind, he and Bram rubbed her shoulders before leading her toward the metal railing that looked down on the lower level. The main floor and the basement were basically two large open spaces. Here was where the tamer public scenes were on display for anyone's viewing pleasure.

Of course, it was debatable if most of the things that went down in this joint could be considered tame. The third and fourth levels housed the private rooms. Again, it was up to the occupants of said rooms how private they wanted to keep their play. Many were more than willing to invite the curious observer or even those who wanted to join in on the action. He and Bram had already decided that no one would be allowed to watch or participate in anything they did with Lacey tonight. Yes, one of the things on her list was public sex—and this place certainly fit that bill—but regardless of what Lacey might argue to the contrary, she wasn't ready to be fucked in a room full of strangers. It was definitely one of those things that worked better if you built up to it over time. If she decided down the road she still wanted to try it, he'd be more than happy to oblige. Hell, not like he had any problem driving her out of her mind with pleasure in front of an appreciative audience. God knows, he'd loved the hell out of it when Bram had been watching.

But tonight a different item was on the menu. One she wasn't aware they'd be checking off—her desire to be tied up and blindfolded. There was one room upstairs that provided an intriguing way to go about it. Bram had called ahead of time to reserve the space as well as to have a few necessities purchased from the club's in-house store sent up to the room.

Lust, hot and heady, pooled in Ry's groin when he imagined Lacey's response to what they had in mind. He glanced toward Bram and caught the fire simmering in his eyes and the telltale flush creeping along his neck. He was just as aroused as Ry at the prospect of what waited for them upstairs.

Ry curled his fingers around Lacey's and pivoted away from the railing. She didn't immediately follow, and he gave her a questioning look. Her focus veered toward the stairway in the opposite direction, the one that led down to the basement level—or the dungeon, as the regulars referred to it. "Aren't we...going down there?"

The last thing he wanted to do was watch those scenes below when his entire body was primed to take her upstairs so they could create their own infinitely more satisfying one. But he couldn't deny her this if it was truly what she desired. Squeezing her hand, he led their trio to the stairs. Once they reached the bottom he waited to see which spectacle would pique Lacey's curiosity. Recessed speakers in the walls provided a nonintrusive loop of electronica music. Its sexy, pulsing beat provided a steady soundtrack for the rhythmic slap of whips and floggers that were being used in the BDSM display. Lacey surprised him by heading in that direction.

A few other spectators were crowded around to watch one of the club's more skilled Doms teach the proper technique for using his implements of choice on the willing participant bent over a metal spanking stand. Ry detected Lacey's hard swallow. Difficult to say if the sound was provoked by the crisscrossing pattern of red stripes marking the woman's ass, or the cuffs bolting the female's hands and feet to the base of the stand.

He looked down and noticed Lacey was staring entranced at the scene. She licked her lips, and another thunderbolt of lust ricocheted through him. His concern that she might be repelled by the sight before her instantly dissolved. No, she was definitely intrigued and aroused. Which only made him more anxious to get her upstairs. Apparently he wasn't the only one because Bram leaned forward and *accidentally* brushed his fingers along Lacey's breast. She jumped slightly, her gaze jerking up to meet Bram's. Ry took advantage of her momentary distraction and squeezed her hand. "Let's go."

She turned toward him, her forehead furrowed with a frown. "We're leaving? Already?"

"No. We have a surprise for you upstairs."

"What kind of surprise?"

He nudged closer to her until his thigh butted against hers. Pressing his mouth near her ear, he flattened her palm over his erection. "The kind you'll like."

A breath shuddered from her, and her fingers reflexively tightened around his cock. Scraping her teeth over her bottom lip, she stroked him through the denim. His rough exhale gusting free, he tugged her away from the display and headed toward the steps. It took every ounce of control he possessed not to sweep Lacey into his arms and barrel up to the room. As it was, he ground his teeth in frustration when they reached the locked door and Bram fumbled around in his wallet for the coded keycard. Finally Bram slipped the card into the slider and swung the door open.

A gasp escaped Lacey as she stepped inside. Although Bram had given him a tour of this room before, Ry tried to see the space from Lacey's perspective. The stone walls were swathed floor to ceiling with black velvet drapes lined with red silk. An oddly shaped leather bench rested near the far wall, its funky design perfect for making love in a variety of positions. Interesting as that piece of furniture was, it didn't hold a candle to the room's main attraction.

Lacey stepped forward, her attention riveted to the large suspension cage and the uniquely engineered harness swing hanging from the center pulley. "W-what's that for?"

Ry stepped behind her and caressed her rib cage. "You."

She gulped. "You're going to strap me into that?"

"Hell yeah." Bram moved in front of Lacey,

sandwiching her between he and Ry. "You're gonna love it. The harness binds you, but the swing makes it feel like you're floating in air."

"Have you used it before?"

"No, but I've always wanted to." Bram relieved Lacey of her coat and tossed it onto one of the nearby chairs before removing his jacket and adding it to hers.

Ry followed suit and unbuttoned Lacey's blouse. He slipped his hands beneath the opened sides and cupped her breasts, massaging their weight through her bra. "This will be a first for all of us."

She nestled against his collarbone and released a shaky sigh. "I'm glad."

He kissed the crown of her head, the sweet floral scent of her hair filling his nose and making him ache. But in a good way. The best way. "Me too."

Bram ducked his head and nibbled along Lacey's jaw before sliding his mouth down the slope of her neck, heading toward the deep V of her cleavage. He groaned. "How about we get rid of these clothes?"

Ry was all for that idea. Leaving Bram to take care of Lacey's boots, pants and G-string bikini, he eased her top off and caressed her shoulders before unhooking her bra and letting it fall to join the rest of her garments. He traced the gentle curve of her spine, his focus drifting to the smattering of freckles that dotted her hip. Stooping, he kissed the tempting marks and massaged her ass cheeks. Unable to resist a second longer, he nipped her butt and smacked it, the action making her squeal. He chuckled.

"Naughty girl. We saw the way you stared at that girl while she was getting spanked. Were you hoping you could take her place?"

"M-maybe."

Her stuttering response provoked a growl from his throat. "No one touches you but Bram or me. But we'd be happy to make that fantasy come true for you, baby."

"Now?"

He bit her again and reveled in her sharp intake of air. "Impatient, aren't we? No, we had some other form of teasing in mind for tonight." He straightened and took her hand while Bram claimed her other. Together they led her to the harness swing and helped her step into the leg restraints. Once those were properly fastened, they secured her into the torso section, making sure that the bindings were snug enough to provide pleasure but not restrict blood flow. By the time they were finished getting her situated, her skin was all flushed and pink and her breaths came in wispy, ragged pants.

"Now what?" An unmistakable tremor of excitement shook her voice.

Bram strode to the small end table where their purchased goodies were laid out. He picked up the silk blindfold and ran it between his fingers. "Now we see exactly how much pleasure you can stand." His grin sinful, he tucked the cloth around Lacey's eyes and knotted it firmly behind her head. "Can you see anything?"

"N-no." Lacey's entire body was quivering now,

making the swing dip and creak. They'd barely touched her and already she was incredibly aroused. Ry could smell the musky evidence of it.

Jesus. He wanted to bury his mouth in her pussy and gorge on her until she was screaming and coming hard on his tongue. His hands unsteady, he fumbled with his black pullover and tugged it off before kicking out of his shoes and stripping from his jeans and briefs. The rustle of clothing hinted that Bram was equally engaged in getting himself naked.

"Why are you guys taking so long? Is this all part of your evil plan to drive me crazy?"

Ry returned to Lacey, keeping his approach stealthy and quiet. He barely grazed his fingertips over her nipples and she jerked. Her lips parted, her breath quickening. Without saying a word, he leaned in and kissed her. His groan floated free as her tongue met his in a lusty joining, and she scraped her nails along his jaw. She gasped for air and he used the opportunity to nuzzle her neck, sucking the soft spot just beneath her ear. She shivered. "Oh God. Ry, that feels so good."

He lifted his head as Bram moved beside him. They both shared a grin, and Bram cleared his throat. "Uh, Lace. That was me."

She snorted. "Nice try. Ry's gone a lot longer in between shaving than you, Mr. Smooth Face."

Bram grunted. "Damn, busted."

Ry gave Lacey's ear a gentle love bite. "Pretty soon you won't be able to cheat by using your hands. Then we'll see how good you are at figuring us out."

"W-what do you mean I won't be able to—" She yelped when Ry cranked the pulley that lowered the head and torso section of the swing. Bram grabbed the ties affixed to the side bars of the suspension cage and fastened them to the leg restraints Lacey wore. The bindings spread her thighs into a wide V, leaving her completely exposed and unable to do a thing about it. The knowledge sent a hot spear of lust through Ry, making his cock bob. He stroked it before reaching for the matching ties that hung loosely from the opposite rails. These came with velvet-lined Velcro cuffs, which he promptly secured around Lacey's wrists. She was now thoroughly at their mercy.

Fuck, this was going to be hot and mind blowing. "Everything okay, baby? None of those straps are digging into you, are they?"

Swallowing hard, she shook her head. He stroked her cheek. "You need to say the words, Lacey. It's important to verbalize if you're enjoying something or not. Bram and I don't want to mistake or miss any cues you might give us. All right?"

She nodded before apparently recalling his orders. "No, I like it. It feels kind of like I'm lying on a hammock." A ghost of a smile tilted her lips. "Make that a hammock used for dirty, kinky sex."

Both he and Bram laughed, but the sound died in Ry's throat as he stepped around Lacey and got his first real view of her pussy on such perfect display. The snug black straps of the harness acted like a frame to her pink, glistening flesh. She was unbelievably wet. Moisture trickled constantly from her slit and slid between the cheeks of her ass. The sound that ripped from Ry was nearly unrecognizable, even to him. His knees hit the carpet and a second later, his tongue plunged inside all that sweet sugar. She cried out, the harness swaying slightly as she writhed. Her bonds significantly limited her motions though. Knowing that she had no choice but to remain open and available to his feasting fueled Ry's hunger to the max. Grasping her hips, he sucked on her clit until the tiny nubbin slickened and swelled.

A stream of incoherent pleas tumbled from Lacey. He knew she was on the brink of coming and desperate for him to push her over the edge. A twinge of guilt shuttled through him at not giving in to her, but his end goal wasn't a fast, merciful orgasm. When she came, it'd be like nothing she'd experienced. So fucking good, there'd be no lingering question in her mind about if this threesome would work. Her head might resist, but her body would see to it that it wouldn't be for long.

Spearing his tongue into her pussy, he fucked her with shallow lashes before probing deeper. Lacey's sobs intensified and her inner channel rippled around him. Her juices coated his mouth, ran down his chin. He slipped his tongue from her and flattened it, plowing through her soaked cleft and along her perineum. When he swirled over her asshole, she bucked in the harness.

"Ry, oh *God*."

He continued lapping at her rosebud, priming himself as much as her. There was no way his cock wasn't getting inside this sweet ass tonight. Judging from Lacey's response to his oral devotion, she wouldn't be likely to tell him no. Lifting his head, he glanced toward her face, his focus roving along her straining body. The crisscrossing straps of the harness plumped her breasts. Her nipples were two firm, erect peaks capping the creamy, generous mounds.

She was as tempting as a candy store fully stocked with every single one of his most favorite treats. He wanted to sample all the delights she had to offer, over and over until he was thoroughly glutted on her. He glanced sideways and noticed Bram's hooded gaze was glued to Lacey's pussy. His fist was squeezing the base of his cock, trying to keep it from blowing. Ry nodded toward the collection of condoms waiting on the table before ducking beneath Lacey's outstretched leg. After kissing her hip, he stood beside her, drinking in the delicious sight she made. "Do you have any idea how damn sexy you are, baby?"

Snagging her lip between her teeth, she shook her head, making her blonde curtain of hair swish from side to side. Her cheeks pinkened. "Sorry, I mean no."

It made him ridiculously pleased that she'd remembered his admonishment about using words rather than gestures. "You are." He skated his palm over her skin, loving the contrast of its silky smoothness compared to the rougher surface of the harness. His fingertips coasted across her nipples just as Bram settled between her legs and began eating her out. The visual was almost too much for Ry to take. Smothering a groan, he left Lacey and went to fetch a condom and a bottle of lube. As he was about to pivot, his eye caught the bulbous-shaped butt plug sitting nearby. Bram hadn't mentioned he'd purchased one.

Mentally sending himself a note to thank Bram for his foresight, Ry swiped the plug too and returned to Lacey. He dropped the lube and condom packet on the floor but held on to the plug as he bent down and flicked Lacey's nipple softly with his tongue before sucking the distended nub into his mouth. She trembled, a broken gasp springing past her lips. He shot a look toward Bram. "No letting her come yet."

Bram gave a wet, muffled response that Ry took to be an affirmative. Ry plucked at Lacey's damp nipple. "Anal is on your list. Have you done it before?"

She licked her lips, her throat working with a swallow. "No."

A primal satisfaction surged through him. The notion that no man had claimed her anal cherry made him all the more determined to be the one to do it. "I want to be your first, baby. Tonight. Are you okay with that?"

She hesitated for a moment. "Yes."

He rubbed his jaw over her breast, relishing the sexy noises she made when his beard scruff tickled her nipple. "I'm going to make it good for you. I promise you won't regret giving me this gift." He placed the plug on her belly so that she would feel it. "I'm going to get you ready for me by using this. While your ass is stretching to accommodate it, I want you to pretend it's my cock filling you. All right?"

She gulped. "Okay." Her voice sounded thin and reedy. He glanced toward Bram, making sure he was keeping his word about not making her come. Bram had stopped licking her and was now using two fingers buried knuckles-deep in her pussy to keep her on the edge.

Ry grabbed the bottle of lube and snatched the plug from its perch on Lacey's stomach. He greased up the device and scooted next to Bram. They both watched, entranced, as Ry squirted a dollop of the lube into Lacey's ass and worked the gel inside with his thumb. A strangled noise came from Lacey, and he immediately stopped. "Am I hurting you?"

"No. *God.* I-It feels...amazing." She shivered.

He removed his thumb and eased the head of the plug in slowly. The resistant ring of muscle protested invasion, but finally he managed to seat the entire plug inside of her. He stared at Lacey stretched so enticingly before him, ass stuffed with a dildo and her pussy hugging Bram's fingers. His cock felt like it was going to explode.

Bram gave a tortured moan. "Fuck. *Must* fuck."

Ry would have chuckled if he weren't thinking the same exact damn thing. He slapped the discarded condom into Bram's hand before hefting to his feet and moving toward the front of the cage. Bending, he snagged the other condom and palmed it. He cupped Lacey's cheek, stroking her as Bram positioned himself between her thighs.

The twin groans that fell from Bram and Lacey as he entered her tightened Ry's balls. Bram withdrew slightly before sinking in again. And again. The slick sound of their lovemaking was the most erotic thing Ry had ever heard. And the look of pure ecstasy on Bram's face almost made him jealous that he wasn't the one pumping in and out of Lacey.

"How does she feel?"

"Fucking amazing." Gripping the straps that supported Lacey's hips and thighs, Bram peered down, his focus glued to where he and Lacey were joined. "All I can feel is wet, snug pussy. So good."

Ry brushed the hair away from Lacey's perspiring forehead. "Tell me what you're feeling, baby."

"Bram's cock. Gliding in me." She shuddered, her body pulling tight. "I don't think anyone's ever been in me this deep before."

I will be. Soon. Ry leaned forward and caressed her breast. "Are you concentrating on the plug in your ass, imagining it's my cock?"

"Y-yes."

"Good." He rolled her nipple between his thumb and forefinger. She kissed the base of his cock before sweeping her tongue along his balls. The sensation made his gut clench and his knees unsteady. Repositioning himself, he gripped his dick and fed her the head. She sucked him in, using her throat muscles to draw him in deeper. Glancing up, he saw that Bram was staring at them. In addition to his glassy-eyed look, the sweat pouring off Bram hinted that he wouldn't last too much longer. Ry fucked Lacey's mouth with two long, luxurious strokes before easing free and untying her arms. While Bram worked the restraints from her ankles, Ry rubbed the circulation back into her hands, pressing a kiss to both her wrists. "I'm going to sit you up now, okay? Be ready for it." He released the pulley that kept her suspended on her back, and she straightened with a gasp.

Bram caught her around the hips, keeping her anchored on his cock. Her arms and legs twined around Bram as he kissed her like a starved man. Ry ripped open the condom packet, his body screaming with the need to fuck Lacey, mark her in some primal way as his. Moving with more determination than grace, he sheathed himself and generously coated his dick with lube. He removed the plug from her ass and nudged his cock inside her, easily stroking deep with one thrust.

Lacey cried out, the ecstatic tremble in the sound verifying that it'd been produced by pleasure rather than pain. His vision hazed and his heart pounded. He cupped her breasts, her nipples straining between his fingers as he fucked her with a raw intensity that blindsided him. He bit the side of her neck and soothed the sting with his tongue. Through the thin membrane dividing Lacey's ass from her pussy, he detected the hard ridge of Bram's cock tunneling into her with equal passion.

Lacey freed one arm from Bram and reached behind her to clasp Ry's hip. "Don't stop," she gasped. "*Please* don't stop."

Bram's agonized features looked like they'd been chiseled from stone. Ry figured his must not be much better. Still, they somehow obeyed her wishes, alternating their strokes so that she was constantly filled. Their rhythm became an unconscious thing—a matching tempo, a syncopated heartbeat. Lacey's fingers dug into Ry's flank, slipping in the sweat he'd built up. He was so tuned to Lacey that he knew the exact moment the orgasm welled within her, even before she verbalized it.

"Oh God, I'm coming."

He pumped deeper, fucking her in short, determined strokes. "Do it, baby. Milk our cocks with your ass and pussy."

Her entire body tensed before bowing into a tight arch. The keening cry that tore from her, along with the way her inner muscles clamped around Ry, sent him over the cliff. He roared, the come jetting from him in fierce spurts, flooding the condom. In that moment, he despised the thin covering of latex that separated him from Lacey, wanting to fill her with his seed. He continued hugging her as Bram's eyes rolled back in his head and his hips jerked, coming with them.

A sense of connection washed over Ry, almost more amazing and fulfilling than his climax. Everything was right. Perfect. The only woman he'd truly wanted, ever loved, was in his arms, sandwiched between him and his best friend—someone who knew all too well exactly what Ry was feeling.

He wondered if it should be illegal to be this happy. Probably. Sliding a kiss along her temple, he gently pulled his cock from her ass and crossed to the wastebasket to dispose of the condom, his legs still shaking from the freight-train force of his orgasm. By the time Ry returned to Lacey, Bram had recovered enough to settle Lacey on her feet and remove her blindfold.

Her body quivering with aftershocks, Lacey blinked at them and offered a grin loaded with sexual satiation. She tugged the straps securing her in the harness. "Wow, all I've got to say is...where the hell can I buy one of these?"

CHAPTER TEN

It was near impossible to act casual and normal during the employee Christmas party when less than twenty-four hours ago she'd been getting double penetrated by the two men standing beside her. In a *swing*, for God's sake.

Okay, she wasn't completely certain if that detail somehow made her more depraved. The fact that she'd loved the hell out of it? Yeah, probably.

Butterflies dancing around in her belly, she watched Donna call up the next staff member for the Secret Santa exchange. This part of the festivities was strictly for the employees. She, Ry and Bram had already passed out everyone's bonus checks, something that was likely more welcome and useful than a ten-dollar-or-under gift.

Ry's cell phone suddenly buzzed, and he glanced down at it. "Shit, it's my uncle. I better go take this."

While Ry ducked out of the room, Bram settled his hand on her shoulder and leaned down to whisper in her ear. "So what item do you want to mark off tonight?"

She knew that even if anyone had overheard him, the question would sound completely innocent. Which would make the blush that was no doubt riding her cheeks seem strange and uncalled for. She cleared her throat quietly. "None. I already made plans with your sister."

His fingers brushed her nape, tickling the fine hairs there and making goose bumps crop along her skin. "You could cancel them. She'd understand."

She snorted. "Please, this is Jana we're talking about. Besides, that would be rude. And my life doesn't revolve around you and Ry, you know."

Bram chuckled, apparently not concerned by her testiness. "Ah, darlin'. Seemed like you were revolving between us just fine last night."

He would have to bring that up. Biting her lip, she resisted the urge to press her legs together when her clit throbbed in response to his smoky words. She hadn't entirely been joking when she'd mentioned buying one of those harness swings. The experience they'd given her in it last night? Talk about out of this world. Of course, it might be a little difficult—not to mention awkward—explaining its function if her parents were to accidentally see it. Somehow she doubted they'd believe her if she said it was a plant stand.

"Earth to Lacey."

She snapped out of her mental musings and peered up at Bram again. "Hmm?"

"I asked where you and Jana are going tonight."

She narrowed her eyes at him. "Nice try. If I tell you, you and Ry will just decide to barge in on us."

Bram tried for an innocent look. "Now would we ever do something so devious?"

"Yes. Hence the reason I'm not telling you jack shit."

Ry chose that moment to rejoin them. "Not tell him what?"

She opened her mouth, but Bram beat her to the punch. "Where my wayward sister is taking her tonight." Bram gave an exaggerated shudder. "I bet it will involve—*gasp*—drinking. And excessive man ogling."

"Har har, Colton. Just for that you can bite me."

Bram waggled his eyebrows. "I would, darlin'. But you're going out tonight. See what you're missing out on?"

She shot a covert look around to see if anyone was paying attention to Bram's overt flirting. Not that it was so unusual. Except he was doing it with *her.* Something that definitely hadn't occurred before they started sleeping together. She was gratified to notice that everyone's attention was focused on the Secret Santa exchange. Ry suddenly cleared his throat. Twice. She glanced in his direction and became ensnared in his penetrating gaze. "What?"

"I think the three of us need to have a powwow in your office."

"Right *now*? But the party—"

"Will continue without us," Ry finished. "Besides, you know they're all waiting for the bosses to leave so they can spike the punch bowl." He inclined his head toward the double doors leading from the Dockside's rear banquet room.

Taking the hint, she led the way out into the hall and to her office. Once they were inside and Bram shut the door, Ry pulled her into his arms and kissed her. Quite thoroughly. By the time he finished, her head was spinning and she was having a hard time remembering their purpose for leaving the party. Her breath ragged, she straightened the lock of hair that'd escaped the butterfly clip anchoring it and shot Ry an accusing stare. "I thought we were coming in here for a powwow, not some bow chicka wow wow."

"We did. But you looked like you needed to be kissed first." He stroked her cheek. "And I wanted to be the one to do it."

The tender yet hot look in Ry's eyes left her feeling all jiggly-kneed and melty inside. She sucked in a deep breath, trying to compose herself. "You guys need to stop affecting me this way at work. It's not helping me in the least."

"I'm glad you brought that up because that's what I wanted to talk to you about." Ry crossed his arms over his chest, the posture equal parts casual and commanding. His assessing gaze drilled into her. "Is there a particular reason you freak out whenever there's a chance someone might look at one of us with you and speculate?"

She blinked at him. "I haven't been freaking out."

"Close enough. You were practically ready to jump out of your skin when Bram teased you seconds ago about biting you."

"Well what did you expect me to do? It's not like any of our staff knows what's going on between us. Or should."

"Why not?"

Ry's calmly worded request nearly knocked her on her ass. "Hello. We're engaged in a threesome. Probably not something we should go public with. Particularly to our employees."

"I'm not suggesting we tell them what's going on. Or anyone else for that matter, unless we choose to. But it doesn't mean we have to keep it hidden like a dark, dirty secret."

She gaped at him. "Won't that defeat the purpose? If we start acting differently with each other, people will figure it out."

Bram stepped next to Ry, providing a united front. "So what if they do? What's the worst that can happen? A few jealous busybodies whisper behind our backs? Hell, I'm used to it."

She swallowed. "Yeah, so am I."

Ry stared at her for a long moment before swearing softly beneath his breath. "This isn't another repeat of what you went through with Dan. Bram and I would never bring that kind of hurt onto you, baby. Believe that."

"Does it matter? In the end, people will see it however they want, just like they did with the Dan fiasco." She despised how her voice cracked on the last two words. She refused to give her ex the power to affect her after all this time.

Bram and Ry crossed the room in two long strides and wrapped her in the middle of their bear hugs. Ry was the first to speak. "I'm sorry. I wasn't even thinking when I brought it up. The last thing I want to do is upset you."

Bram nuzzled the back of her head. "That goes double for me, Lace. What the three of us share—it's special. I don't want to lose it. If that means keeping my mouth shut, I'll gladly do it."

His proclamation should have made her happy. So why did she feel so awful inside? *Because you're asking them to live a lie.* The taunting admission churned her stomach and made her feel like the most terrible person on the planet. But it didn't lessen her determination to protect herself from the inevitable fallout that would come once their sexy adventures came to a close. No one would criticize Ry and Bram for their part in this affair. Being men, they could get away with a lot more than her when it came to having multiple bed partners. Yes, it was hugely unfair. But it was also reality.

In this regard, at least, fantasy definitely had its advantages. No painful repercussions could come from sex that only existed in her head.

Lacey was just popping her earrings in when her front doorbell rang. She glanced at her watch, surprise flickering over her. How unlike Jana to actually be on time for once.

After indulging in a quick spritz of perfume, she hurried down the hall and swung open the door as the chime went off again. She gave Jana a frazzled look. "You do realize you're supposed to wait at least a few seconds in between pressing that thing, right?"

"Sorry, but it's freakin' cold out here. I can't even feel my ass anymore." Jana reached behind herself and smacked her butt through her leather trench coat. "Yep, nothing. I'm assuming it's still back there."

"Part of your problem is your coat. It has hardly any lining."

Jana offered a cheeky grin. "I know, but my ma insists it makes me look like a streaker. I find that kinda amusing."

"You would. So are you driving or me?"

"I will. Heat's already on." Jana pivoted and clunked down the driveway in her combat boots. Lacey quickly locked up her house and hurried toward Jana's vintage Mustang. As promised, the interior was toasty warm. That slightly made up for having to listen to several tracks of the Chipmunks' Christmas album before they pulled into the packed lot of Hooligans. She gave Jana a pointed look as the CD ejected from the player. "I'm pretty sure it's illegal for anyone over the age of twelve to own that CD. If not, it should be."

Sticking out her tongue, Jana climbed from the car and waited for Lacey to do the same before beeping the alarm. Linking arms, they dashed toward the entrance of the nightclub, giggling like a couple of teenage girls out on a school night. After paying their cover charges at the door, they made their way to the massive bar situated in the middle of the jam-packed building.

Jana wiggled out of her coat, revealing a skintight micro minidress in a tartan plaid fabric. When she hopped onto one of the available stools, half the men sitting at the bar craned their necks hoping to see exactly how much thigh she'd end up revealing. Jana—being her typical couldn't-give-a-shit self—ignored them all.

Feeling significantly overdressed in her cream-colored slacks and red, glittery top, Lacey took the neighboring stool and tried not to grin at the poor shmuck next to Jana who seemed to be hypnotized by her cleavage. "You really should come with a warning label—*might create whiplash when in public.*"

"Please. This is one of my tamer outfits. And I'm actually wearing underwear."

"Your mom must be so proud."

"Very." Putting two fingers in her mouth, Jana gave an ear-piercing whistle that probably had dogs from miles away baying in agony. It barely cracked a glance from the bartender working farther down the way. Jana grumbled. "This place sucks donkey balls. Tell me why they wouldn't have more than one bartender? Idjits."

"Yeah, it is pretty stupid. A night like this, we always have at least two on staff at the Dockside. And we never see crowds like they have here."

"Speaking of idjits, how'd my brother take the news

about me stealing you away tonight? And Ry, for that matter."

The mention of Bram and Ry stirred up Lacey's earlier troubled thoughts. She tried her best to cover it, but Jana's shrewd focus narrowed on her. "Uh-oh. Trouble in ménage land already?"

"No, of course not. Everything's...great."

Jana arched a brow. "But?"

"Nothing. I said it's great."

"Sure, after you hesitated."

Needing something to occupy her hands, Lacey grabbed one of the beverage napkins from the nearby stack and fiddled with it.

"Are you going to answer my question or make an origami stork?"

Lacey crumpled the napkin in her lap. "I think I hurt their feelings by insisting we keep our threesome under wraps."

Jana's husky laugh belted out in all its unrestrained glory. "Right. I don't think that's even possible with Bram—Mr. Love 'em and Leave 'em. As far as Ry...hmm, not sure. But I doubt he's crying in his SpaghettiOs."

"I don't know." The same twisting sensation she experienced earlier in her stomach returned. "For some reason, I feel like I've let them down."

"Okay, then come out of the closet and admit to everyone that the three of you are sleeping together."

Lacey winced at the loudness of Jana's voice. Thank God she didn't know anyone in this place. "I already told you I'm not doing that."

"Oh that's right. Because you think this is only a temporary fling." There was no mistaking the heavy sarcasm in Jana's tone.

Lacey glared at her. "Yes, it is."

"Bullshit." Jana cocked her finger warningly when Lacey opened her mouth. "You know it is. Girl, you can tell me until you're blue in the face that you're the kind to indulge in kinky affairs, but it won't make it true."

"Okay, if you know so much, then *you* tell me what this is."

"Love."

That single word packed one hell of a punch. Lacey reeled from it, her fingers digging into the roll of leather stitching ringing the stool. "*What?*"

The fierceness in Jana's eyes mellowed. "It's okay. You can admit that you love them. I've known it for a while."

"Really? Then you know a hell of a lot more than I do." She caught the stubborn glint returning to Jana's gaze and held up a hand. "All right. I can see how you'd think that. I'm always spending a lot of time around them." *Because they make me happy like no one else.* "We own a business together. It's to be expected."

"You guys have been inseparable for a lot longer than you've owned the Dockside."

"Because we're friends."

"Friends who are now fucking each other," Jana pointed out bluntly.

It was on the tip of Lacey's tongue to correct her and say it was more than just sex, but she knew Jana would take it the wrong way. Just because she felt an emotional bond with Ry and Bram every time they came together didn't mean she was in love with them.

Did it?

The twisting intensified in her stomach. "This isn't about love." It couldn't be. That path only led to pain. She'd tried it once before and ended up burned. Big time. It wouldn't happen again. "It's about rediscovering my sexuality. Indulging in a fantasy that plenty of women out there have. It's nothing more than that."

Jana continued eyeing her for a long stretch, her expression skeptical. "I think you're fooling yourself."

The bartender chose that moment to finally show up with the drink menus. Lacey accepted one, grateful for the much-needed reprieve from Jana's persistent grilling.

She only wished she could get a similar respite from the worried doubts brewing in her head.

CHAPTER ELEVEN

"If there was one thing I'd hoped to never see in my lifetime, it was Santa in a Speedo." Grimacing, Lacey turned away from the spectacle of the white-haired, potbellied patron gyrating on the dance floor in the tight red spandex swimsuit. This was one of the pitfalls of hosting a beach-themed party during the Christmas season. "Would someone please go get a towel for that guy?"

"I'm on it, boss." Dwayne, one of the busboys, hurried in the direction of the giant umbrella in the corner. Thank God they'd decided to use beach towels in the display.

Bram stepped out of his and Ry's office and slung his arm around her shoulder. "Wow, look at Santa shaking his Rudolph."

She stifled a groan. "Way to ruin my favorite reindeer for me."

"I try, darlin'. I try."

She glanced toward the closed door behind them. "Is Ry still on the phone with his uncle?"

"Yeah. He's attempting to wrap it up, but it might be a while."

Holidays were tough for Charlie Hollister since he'd lost his wife on Christmas Day ten years ago. She knew that Ry felt incredibly guilty not being able to spend more time with his uncle, despite knowing that his cousins were there to watch over Charlie day and night and ensure that the depression didn't result in him holing up in his house. "He's a good nephew."

"I was thinking of suggesting the three of us pop in on Charlie sometime before Christmas Day. That's if you don't mind."

She squeezed Bram's hand. "That's a wonderful idea. Count me in."

Bram stared at her for a long moment without saying anything. Unsettled by the intensity in his eyes, she nibbled her lip. "What is it? Do I have something stuck in my teeth?" *Damn spinach salad.*

"No." He glanced toward the bar before lowering his voice. "You have no idea how damn much I want to kiss you right now."

"Oh." Her gaze slipped to Bram's lips, and she imagined their firm pressure upon hers, the coaxing glide of his tongue.

"Christ, Lace. If you keep looking at me like that, I'm gonna want to do a lot more than kiss you. Right here with everyone watching."

She took a shuddering breath before refocusing on the revelers partying on the dance floor. Bram's fingers trailed down her spine and lingered near her tailbone, dangerously close to dipping into the crease of her ass. "Come home with us tonight. We can relax in the hot tub. Drink some wine. Fall in bed together and fuck like rabbits."

She gave a shaky laugh. "You really know how to tempt a gal."

"Is that a yes?"

She nodded. "But only because I'm dying to soak in the hot tub."

His grin let her know that she didn't have him fooled.

Three hours later, Bram's tongue was inside her mouth, delivering the lush, blistering kiss he'd enticed her with back at the Dockside. Meanwhile, Ry's tongue was swirling over her clit. They hadn't even made it out of the entryway of Bram's house. Gasping, she dug her fingers into Bram's shoulders, holding on for dear life as a fierce, unexpected orgasm swept her up in its riptide. She cried out, her thighs reflexively clamping around Ry's head. He groaned, each tug of his lips, teeth and tongue extending the beating pulse of her climax until she thought she'd pass out from the overwhelming pleasure of it.

Weak and incredibly sated, she slumped back on the rug with a satisfied sigh. "That. Was. Amazing."

Ry and Bram both chuckled and stroked her arms and

legs. Bram nuzzled her neck, his teeth nipping her lightly. "Does this mean you're not mad about having to wait an extra few minutes for the hot tub?"

"Keep giving me orgasms like that and I'll never be mad again. About *anything.*"

"Deal," Bram and Ry said in unison. While Bram went to get the hot tub ready, Ry stretched over her and claimed her mouth. She could taste herself on his tongue. The reminder of what he'd been doing to her seconds ago triggered a renewed spiral of desire. She twined her arms around him, holding him close. The familiar emotional rush seized her, making her tremble.

Ry lifted his head and looked at her. His fingertips traced her cheek. "Thank you."

She giggled. "Um, shouldn't I be the one saying that right now?"

He rubbed his nose over hers, his rumbling laugh vibrating beneath her hands. "I was referring to you coming over tonight."

She ruffled her fingers through the ends of his hair, and he closed his eyes, his contented moan leaking free. The lines of fatigue furrowed in his forehead softened. "That feels good. I love the way you touch me."

"I love touching you." She gently raked her nails down the nape of his neck, making him shiver. Something squeezed around her heart, the constriction both sweet and terrifying.

This was about sex. Nothing more.

"Hey, you guys coming?" Bram called from the back of

the house.

Grateful for the much-needed distraction from the emotion cramping her chest, Lacey let Ry help her to her feet. Twining their fingers together, he walked with her to the rear deck, where a dense cloud of steam rose from the bubbling hot tub recessed in the teak decking. A buck-naked Bram was busy shoveling a path through the freshly fallen snow. Fortunately a tall privacy fence blocked his neighbors' view of his backyard.

She shook her head in amused disbelief. "He's freaking nuts."

Ry snorted. "You're just now figuring that out?" He quickly shucked his own clothes and took her hand again. "Ready to make a dash for it?"

Considering it had to be no more than twenty degrees out, a leisurely pace was out of the question. Steeling herself, she nodded. Ry shoved open the door and swept her up into his arms, gallantly saving her feet from the snow-packed deck. The brisk chill that instantly enveloped her still made her teeth chatter. Not dilly-dallying, Ry hoofed it down the cleared path and lowered her into the swirling depths of the hot tub before hopping in after her. His blissful groan echoed hers. "Damn, I'm never getting out of this thing."

She sank deeper into the tub, letting the hot, muscle-relaxing water ease away her cares. After stacking some towels on the nearby stand, Bram climbed into the tub with them. She moved over into the molded seat, making room for him, and ended up positioned squarely in front of one of the jets. A constant stream of air bubbles bobbed between her legs. The sensation acted like a sensual powder keg to her already over-primed body. She bit back a moan and wiggled, but that only seemed to make things worse. Sexy chuckles floated from Ry and Bram, hinting that they knew precisely the torment she was going through.

A second later, Bram's hand brushed along her thigh. "What's the matter, darlin'? Bubbles feeling a little too good?" His fingers combed through the curls covering her mound before teasing over her clit. Unable to help it, she arched into his touch, her eyes fluttering shut as the pleasure built to a fever pitch. Bram's mouth closed around the sensitive juncture where her jaw and neck met, the lazy motion of his fingers never losing their persuasive rhythm. Her toes curled and her body bucked under the unrelenting wave of the orgasm that slammed into her.

Bram wrapped an arm around her waist, holding her through the ceaseless quakes. Dimly she heard splashing. She dragged her eyes open to see Ry fumbling through the pile of towels. A second later he held up his prize—a condom packet. His dark, determined gaze locked with hers, he ripped the foil open with his teeth and made short work of sheathing his breath-stealing erection. He plowed through the water toward them and stooped to plunder her mouth, his tongue thrusting inside in an assertive glide that made her pussy clench. All she could think about was being impaled on his cock, losing herself to the ecstasy it could deliver.

As if he'd read her mind, Ry broke the kiss and nipped her earlobe with a growl. "I'm going to bury myself so deep inside you, you're going to be feeling me for the next week."

His husky promise coaxed a renewed flurry of tremors through her body. She wrapped her legs around him, but he surprised her by unhooking them from his hips and lifting her from the seat. His purpose became clear when he faced her away from him and toward Bram, who had hefted himself onto the edge of the hot tub. Steamy rivulets of water streamed down Bram's abdomen and matted the trim patch of hair nestled at the base of his straining cock. She took one look at his glistening shaft and began salivating. With a hungry groan, she leaned forward and engulfed him in one downstroke of her mouth. The muscles in Bram's six pack became even more defined as they tensed. He gripped the ledge of the tub, his knuckles whitening.

Ry widened her stance before positioning his cock against her slit. "Put your arms around him, baby. You need something to hold on to because I'm going to fuck you hard."

She moaned, the sound muffled by Bram's cock. Dutifully she obeyed Ry's command. No sooner did she grasp Bram's waist when Ry slammed into her, sinking to the hilt in one powerful thrust. His pistoning hips pinned her to the side of the hot tub, aligning her pussy with the pulsating jet. The intense vibrations beating against her clit combined with the thick, rock-hard shaft hammering into her slick flesh hurtled her into a place where coherent thought no longer existed. Her world narrowed down to the two cocks claiming total possession of her. In this moment, she no longer owned her body. They did.

Sucking Bram deeper, she looked up to find him watching the motions of her mouth. Moonlight silvered his eyes, making him appear mysterious. And incredibly sexy. She swallowed, working him with her throat muscles. He tipped his head back, the cords in his neck straining. The need to make him come was overwhelming. She wanted to see the pleasure washing over his face while his seed spurted down her throat. The desperate desire to feel and hear Ry lost in his own orgasm was no less consuming.

Releasing one arm from Bram's waist, she cupped his balls, massaging them softly as she bobbed her head faster. His thighs tensed, a ragged groan tearing from him. She lifted her hips slightly, knowing Ry would now feel the full force of the jets. His thrusts faltered before doubling in intensity. She sobbed around Bram's cock, struggling to defeat the insistent ripples luring her toward climax. Ry fucked her harder, deeper, his silent demand louder than words. They wouldn't come without her falling into the abyss first.

She gave herself over to the orgasm, giving it full rein to shatter through her and break her into a million pieces. Her reward was Ry and Bram's echoing shouts of ecstasy as their cocks emptied inside her. Her glow of completion cocooned her in a comforting haze of contentment.

Sex this amazing didn't have a damn thing to do with love. It was all based on body chemistry. And two men who knew every trick in the book to get her off, and weren't afraid to use them. But even as Ry scooped her from the water and passed her into Bram's outstretched arms, Jana's accusing tone ghosted through Lacey's mind.

I think you're fooling yourself.

CHAPTER TWELVE

Joy and happiness bubbled inside Bram as he soaped Lacey's back while Ry took care of her front. Their fingers met between her legs and she moaned.

"Do you two *ever* get tired of sex?"

Bram chuckled. "Don't count on it. At least not when it comes to you, darlin'." He couldn't think of anything he wanted to do more than spend the rest of his days loving her every way he could.

"Well as much as I hate to say no to a potential orgasm, I promised your sister we'd swing by Wicked Delights this morning and pick up her contribution to our toy drive before heading out to cut down your Christmas tree."

A wicked devil riding his shoulder, Bram smacked her left butt cheek, making her squeal. He grinned. "Excellent idea. Ry and I can buy *you* a toy while we're at it."

She snorted. "Why do I get the feeling mine won't be a

teddy bear?"

The three of them took turns rinsing beneath the spray before stepping from the shower and toweling off. He and Ry tried their damnedest to coax Lacey into a little hanky-panky instead of getting dressed right away, but her determination to arrive at Jana's within the hour wouldn't be thwarted. So with his cock throbbing like a motherfucker, he climbed into the backseat of Ry's F250 and buckled up.

The drive to Wicked Delights went by fast, mostly because Ry and Lacey insisted on teasing him the whole way about his long-standing tradition of waiting till the last minute to get his tree. He held up his hands in defense. "Hey, when you're able to get a seven-foot blue spruce for less than twenty bucks, then you can mock."

"Hmm, would it have to be one that actually holds its needles for longer than a day?" Lacey shot back as she reached for her door handle.

"You're never going to let me live that down, are you?"

Ry pocketed his keys. "Nope."

They all climbed out and made their way to the shop. Jana looked up from the selection of sheer teddies she was folding as they stepped inside. "Oh good. I wasn't sure you'd remember." She hurried toward the stockroom, presumably to grab her donation for the toy drive.

Bram strode to the display his sister had been arranging and picked up one of the flimsy negligees. His brows waggled as he held it against the front of Lacey's coat. "Hell, you might be getting a teddy after all."

She rolled her eyes. Despite her refusal to laugh at his incredibly brilliant joke, he searched through the lingerie for the right size. The pink mesh would look and feel incredible against her skin. He was already getting hard thinking about her modeling it. Jana returned to the register with a large, gift-wrapped package. Lacey started to head in that direction, but he tucked her hand in his and swung her around, leading her toward the section of the shop that carried the more risqué items. Ry had beaten them to the aisle, and judging from the collection of goodies stacked in his arms, he'd been making good use of his time.

Lacey's eyes widened. "What'd you do? Pick out one of everything?"

Ry grinned. "Just trying to support Jana's business." His gaze fell on the teddy in Bram's hand. "Mm, nice. You should try it on."

Bram cleared his throat. "Thanks, but I've been told pink isn't my color."

"Smartass." Ry snatched the lingerie from him and handed it to Lacey before steering her toward the fitting rooms. He and Bram piled into the cramped space with her, earning another of her exasperated eye rolls.

"You both could have waited outside, you know."

Bram sat on the edge of the provided bench. Crossing his booted feet in front of him, he leaned back against the wall. "Sure, but where's the fun in that?"

His pronouncement became confirmed when Ry

began undressing Lacey in the sexiest strip show Bram ever had the pleasure of witnessing. *Day-um.* Just seeing Ry's hands trailing over Lacey's creamy skin was enough to get his blood pumping. Bram reached for his fly and adjusted himself.

Ry's palm glided along the inner curve of her calf as she stepped into the teddy. With tormentingly slow movements, he inched the garment into place. As Bram had suspected, the peek-a-boo mesh looked fucking incredible on her. His breath hissed between his teeth. "Jesus."

A hint of worry clouded Lacey's eyes. "What? Do I look ridiculous?"

Bram gave his head a fierce shake. "Hell no. You look more delicious than cotton candy." He licked his lips, already picturing her melting on his tongue.

Ry scooted back on his heels, his expression hinting that he shared a similar mental image as Bram. He reached around Lacey and grabbed one of the goodies he'd brought along with him before digging into his jacket pocket and pulling out the Swiss Army knife he always carried on his person.

Lacey eyed the knife warily. "Uh, should I be worried right now?"

"I'll leave that for you to decide." His eyes flashing with devilment, Ry cut through the outer packaging of the small bullet vibrator.

Lacey frowned. "I don't think Jana's going to

appreciate you opening the merchandise before you purchase it."

"I've got over two hundred dollars worth of stuff here. Trust me, she won't complain." Ry eased aside the crotch of the teddy. When Lacey caught on to his intention, she tried to clamp her thighs shut. Chuckling, he wedged his other arm between her legs, effectively hindering her attempt. He ducked his head and kissed her sweet spot. Lacey bit her lip and trembled. Her quivering turned into a shake when Ry began tonguing her slit. It took all the willpower Bram possessed not to free his cock and begin stroking it. Giving her clit a final lick, Ry slipped the vibrator into her pussy. Humming in approval, he tugged the teddy back in place and patted Lacey's mound before snagging her jeans from the floor.

"Ry..."

"Hm, baby?"

She gaped at him. "Surely you don't expect me to go out like this?"

"That's precisely what I plan." Ignoring her grumbles, Ry helped her get dressed. While she stalked slightly bowlegged from the fitting room, Ry held up the wireless remote for the vibrator. "Remind me to buy batteries from Jana."

Bram bit back a laughing groan. Fuck, this was going to be the best—and *hardest*—morning of his life.

They joined Lacey at the register, and Jana sized up the purchases Ry dumped in front of her, obvious dollar signs tumbling around in her head. Bram noticed that his sister's lips quirked as she took in the opened bullet vibrator package, but surprisingly she kept her sassy mouth shut. "Will this complete your order?"

"No, I'm also wearing one of those." Her cheeks pinker than the teddy under her clothes, Lacey pointed toward the display Bram had swiped the garment from.

"All righty then." Jana's eyes twitching from the effort of holding in her mirth, she rang up the sale.

Bram tried to pass his share of the moolah to Jana, but Ry scooped up the cash and tucked it back in Bram's palm. Ry's mouth curled at one corner. "I believe an arsenal of vibrators trumps your turtle charm. Better luck next Christmas."

Bram chuckled. "Well played, you crafty bastard."

While Jana swiped Ry's credit card she gave Bram an odd look. She glanced briefly at Lacey, who was whispering something in a heated undertone to Ry. No doubt Lace was demanding to know what the batteries were for.

Jana returned her focus to him. "I need to talk to you. Alone."

"Okay. You have my cell phone number. But we're leaving now to go get a tree. Probably better to call me later tonight."

"No. Now. It'll only take a minute."

Shrugging, he gestured for Lacey and Ry to head out to the truck without him. Once they were gone, Jana got right to the point. One that he hadn't been expecting.

Certainly not from his hell-on-wheels sister. "I hope you know what you're doing, playing these sex games with Lacey."

"What do you mean?"

She folded her arms over her Betty Boop T-shirt. "You and I both know how vulnerable she is to getting hurt."

Anger sliced through him. "You think that's what Ry and I want to do? Hurt her? That's the most fucking stupid thing I've ever heard."

"I know you wouldn't *mean* to. But it's almost inevitable, don't you think? For God's sake, she's in love with you guys."

He stared at her, and Jana clamped a hand over her mouth, only to drop it a second later with an, "Oh shit."

His heart began beating in triple time. "Did she tell you that?"

"No, but I always figured. She's in major denial over it though." She winced. "Why can't I shut up? It's like I have Tourette's." She sent him a pleading look. "Let's pretend we never had this conversation, okay?"

Yeah, not fucking likely. "No problem." He shoved his wallet into his rear pocket. "You gonna be at Ma and Pop's Christmas Eve?"

"Of course."

He started to back away from the register, but Jana's pointed cough stalled him short. Her expression was more worried than ever. "Be careful with her heart."

He didn't bother to answer. Like there was any need. He'd sooner saw off his own leg than hurt Lacey. Zipping his jacket, he pivoted and exited the store. As he strode to the truck his chaotic thoughts spun like an endless reel.

Could it be true? Was Lacey in love with them? The possibility made his heart soar. Until he remembered Jana's claim about Lacey being in denial over it. If so, that hinted at the possibility that Lacey was deliberately ignoring what her heart was telling her.

Why?

Everything inside him hungered to corner Lacey and demand if Jana's suspicions were true, after which he'd reassure Lacey that she didn't have to worry about him loving her back. The exact opposite. He loved her so damn much he was ready to explode from the force of his feelings.

But he was also petrified of moving too fast with Lacey. Or worse, scaring her off completely. Dragging his hands down his face, he tugged open the truck's rear passenger door and climbed onto the backseat. Other than Lacey's labored breaths, the front of the vehicle was quiet. He opened his mouth, intending to ask what was going on, but then he noticed the way she was squirming in place, her nails digging into her seat's leather armrests. A gasp broke from her lips, and she squeezed her legs together.

Holy fuck. Ry must be using the remote on her. Bram glanced toward Ry and noticed his ghost of a smile. Ry's hand came out of his pocket, and Lacey let out a relieved breath, her posture immediately relaxing.

Ry shifted out of park. "Who's ready to go tree

hunting?"

Bram smothered a groan. Something told him this was going to be a long afternoon.

But damn if it wasn't gonna be fun.

CHAPTER THIRTEEN

"What about this one?" Trying to keep her balance, Lacey hiked through the ankle-deep fresh powder dusting the thicker crust of old snow. She reached the good-sized evergreen just as a flurry of vibrations kicked through the silver bullet lodged in her pussy. Gritting her teeth, she rode out the tantalizing waves, hoping against hope that they'd last long enough this time to do something more than add to the already-soaked conditions of her crotch.

She panted, swaying. Despite the cold, a trickle of sweat slid toward her cleavage. The vibrations stopped. *Damn them.*

Her two tormenters came into view, and she glared them down. "Which one of you bastards did that?"

They both offered her innocent smiles. Bram's attention drifted to the tree she'd called them over to see. "That's a Fraser fir."

She tossed her arms out. "What freaking difference

does it make?"

"I always get a blue spruce."

It was tempting to weep. Honest to God. Instead she resorted to more crankiness. "You suck."

"Not yet. But we're going to, baby." Ry's gaze smoldered. "I bet your clit's swollen and juicy for us, isn't it?"

Just him asking sent another series of throbbing pulses through the aching bundle of nerves. Who needed a vibrator when she had Ry's smoky voice talking dirty sweet nothings to her?

She stalked forward and wrenched the handsaw from Bram's grasp. "You're getting a fucking Fraser fir." She swiveled toward the tree but managed no more than one step before the bullet went off again. "*Ahhh.*" Her legs wobbling, she dropped the saw. Bram retrieved it and the vibrations stopped. She glared at his broad back. "Sneaky, Colton. You do realize I'm going to make you suffer unbearably for this."

"Trust me, darlin'. I already am."

They spent another fifteen minutes searching for Bram's nonexistent perfect tree. By the time he settled on a six-foot spruce with a mostly asymmetrical shape, she was ready to rip her clothes off and beg them to fuck her. In the snow. Yeah, she'd probably freeze her ass off— literally—but at this rate she wasn't going to quibble. While Bram and Ry took turns sawing through the evergreen's thick trunk, she jogged in place, both out of patience and in the pathetic hope that maybe she'd somehow accidentally trigger the bullet into going off again and giving her the orgasm she so desperately needed.

Finally the tree toppled over, and Ry and Bram each grabbed an end with their gloved hands and carried it toward the path where the tractor-powered wagon would pick them up and take them back to the main lot. The second they dropped the heavy spruce onto the ground, Bram grimaced. "I've got to take a leak."

While Bram tromped back in the direction they just came from, she hurried in front of Ry, her hands clasped together in supplication. "Give me ten seconds with the remote. That's all I'm asking."

He chuckled. "Only ten seconds, huh?"

"I probably don't even need that long."

He seemed to mull it over for a moment. "I've got a counteroffer for you. I'll keep the remote, but I promise I'll leave it on long enough that you'll come."

She was past the point of caring who pushed the button that would ultimately get her off. "Deal."

Ry leaned down until his warm breath puffed a scant inch away from her lips. "Shall we seal it with a kiss?"

She flung her arms around his neck and crushed her mouth over his. Their tongues collided before dancing together in a seductive glide. She wiggled against him, trying to devour him whole, her entire body primed for the lusty, uninhibited loving she so desperately craved. Her teeth scraped his bottom lip as he pulled back with a ragged exhale. He stared at her with a somebody's-gonna-get-fucked-hard glint in his eyes.

Oh *God*, she hoped so.

Bram rejoined them, his insulated boots crunching through the snow. "Any sign of the wagon yet?"

Ry shook his head. She eyed him, waiting for the vibrations that should hit.

Any.

Moment.

Now.

The seconds continued to tick by, and she cleared her throat. Ry glanced her way. All traces of his previous carnal hunger had been wiped clean, replaced instead by the phoniest innocent expression she'd ever witnessed on a human being.

If she'd had a blunt object handy, she would have clubbed him with it. "What are you waiting for?"

He cocked his head, seemingly listening for something. Bram stepped around the trunk of the spruce, his attention fused to the rutted path. "Hey, I think the wagon's coming."

Ry's gaze returned to her. "So it is." And just like that, his angelic demeanor shifted. The smile that stretched his mouth prompted endless goose bumps along her skin.

The big John Deere tractor rumbled into view, the attached canopied wagon bouncing behind it. Sexual frustration welling inside her, she lasered a hot glare at Ry. "You are such a liar."

"No, baby. I fully intend to keep my word. I just never

said when I'd do it."

"How convenient."

The tractor's puttering engine grew louder as the vehicle approached. The wickedness riding Ry's features kicked up several notches, making her nervous. Why did it feel like she'd possibly made a deal with the devil? "Ryan Hollister, what do you have up your sleeve, damn it?"

With a grinding of brakes, the tractor jolted to a halt and its coverall-wearing operator swung down from the top seat. "Howdy."

The bullet began buzzing in her pussy. Biting the inside of her cheek to keep from gasping, she jerked her gaze to Ry and noticed the sparkle in his eyes.

Getting tossed into a pit of alligators would be too merciful for the rotten son of a bitch. No, the death she had planned for him would be slow and excruciating.

"Wow, looks like you folks found yourselves a beauty." Planting his hands on his thighs, the wagon operator stooped to get a better look at the spruce.

The vibrations intensified a fraction.

Oh shit. The damn remote came with different settings? She was so fucked.

God, if only.

Trying to hide her whimpers with a tuneless hum, she shuffled in place. That action only resulted in the crotch of the teddy rubbing between her labia, adding an extra layer onto her torment.

"Let me get you all a tag." The worker fumbled in the

pocket stitched to the front of his bib. His bushy mustache drooped low as he frowned. "Well shoot. Musta left them in the cab." His motions slow and lumbering as a polar bear, he waddled toward his tractor. The pulsations in her pussy lessened. She wanted to scream. Cry. Rip off her pants and demand Ry and Bram fuck her.

"What's the matter, baby? You look a little flushed." His lips twitching, Ry kneaded her shoulder.

She lowered her voice to a fierce whisper that she prayed the tractor driver couldn't hear. "You better be prepared to fuck my brains out when we get home."

The fire in his eyes threatened to burn her alive. "Believe me, that's a given."

She shivered, as much from the sinful promise in his tone as the bullet jiggling in her pussy.

"Here we go." The worker returned with the tag and hunkered to his knees in order to affix it to the spruce. "You boys need a hand hauling this into the wagon?"

"No, we've got it covered." Bram crouched and grabbed the trunk. The vibrations blessedly ceased as Ry stepped around her and wrestled with the front end of the tree. After some grunting and cursing, they situated the evergreen near the back of the wagon. She clambered up the wooden plank steps and plunked her fanny onto one of the prickly bales of hay used for seating. The strong, bracing scent of pine surrounded her, making her feel like she was in the middle of a forest. Oh right, she was. Duh. Being deprived of orgasm was apparently slowly killing off her brain cells. Feeling suitably grouchy, she sent Ry and Bram a peeved look while they sat down on either side of her.

The worker popped his head through the opening. "Everyone ready back here?"

Ry squeezed her knee as the bullet started up again. "More than ready."

Giving the thumbs-up sign, the driver moseyed to the John Deere. Lacey let out a frustrated gasp and swatted at Ry's hand. "You are *such* a bastard."

"No, baby. I'm marking off your wish list. You said you wanted public sex, well I'm giving you a small taste of it." Ry's fingers swept small, distracting figure eights over the denim covering her leg. "Be glad it's as cold as it is. Otherwise I'd be tempted to ruck these jeans down right now and bury my mouth between your legs while that vibe is doing its thing."

Bram leaned forward, his stare moving to her lap. "Holy shit. Don't tell me the bullet's been buzzing this whole time."

"Mostly." Ry's palm smoothed along her clenched thigh. "Just enough to keep her busy wondering if she'd come apart in front of our friend up there." He nodded his chin toward the driver, who was whistling off key in the cab of the tractor. The vehicle lurched forward, jostling them slightly on the bales of hay.

Ry's gloved fingers continued wandering along the inner seam of her jeans until they rested against her crotch. The vibrations increased in tempo. "It's exactly two minutes until we reach the parking lot. I timed it earlier. Think you can come before that, baby? Because I'm warning you right now, we're not going to let up on you until you do."

She was too dazed to completely comprehend Ry's meaning. Even when he used his teeth to yank off his glove she didn't really get it. It wasn't until he unzipped her jeans and slid his hand inside the narrow opening in the denim that his intention pierced the sensual fog clouding her brain. She barely had time to register the blissful stroking of Ry's calloused fingers on her clit before Bram's hand snuck inside her coat and beneath her sweater. His warm palm infinitely arousing, Bram massaged her breast through her bra, his thumb rolling over her nipple. She gasped, her hips jerking. Her pussy clenched around the throbbing bullet, but the climax still hovered out of reach.

The wagon's wheels seemed to hit every rut in the path, bouncing her in a way that did nothing to help her situation. Her desperate moan leaked free before she could stop it. Pulse thundering, she shot a look toward the driver, uncertain if he'd heard.

"One minute, baby, and he'll stop this wagon and walk back here. Know what he'll see?" Ry's mouth pressed against her ear, his beard scruff an erotic scrape along her cheek. "You, coming all over my hand."

Her breath snagged in her throat, excitement and panic jockeying for the foremost sensation in her body. Bram eased down the cup of her bra and plucked her nipple lightly as his teeth grazed the side of her neck. "I wish I was buried inside you right now. Then he'd see you coming all over my cock instead."

She whimpered. Ry's fingers moved in tighter and tighter little circles on her clit. "Does that excite you, naughty girl? Maybe we should give you what you really want."

A tremble began low in her belly.

"What is it that you really want, Lace?" Bram's lips traversed her jaw.

The tractor crossed the metal grate marking the south entrance to the lot. In the not-too-far distance, she could hear the roar of the chainsaws putting cleaner cuts on the customers' trees. The bullet buzzed at maximum speed and velocity. Ry tugged her clit between his thumb and index finger, mimicking the pattern of the vibrations in her pussy. She gasped her answer. "B-both of you."

Ry held her clit firm, not caressing, not stroking, ensuring she felt every echoing beat of the bullet whizzing inside her. "Doing what?"

"Fucking me." The orgasm crashed into her, ripping a startled cry from her that fortunately became quickly muffled by Bram's devouring mouth. Her body shook and convulsed. If not for the security of Ry and Bram's strong arms surrounding her, keeping her steady and upright, she would have melted into a mindless puddle on the floor of the wagon.

The bullet shut off and the quakes ebbed. Ry removed

his fingers and licked them with a hungry groan before zipping her jeans. By the time the wagon shuddered to a halt, Bram had straightened her bra and buttoned her coat back up. Other than her breath wheezing from her a little too fast, no one would be the wiser of what they'd been up to. But the realization of how close they'd come to being caught only ratcheted the exhilarated thrill racing through her.

Holy crap. Never in her wildest imaginings would she have believed she'd have the guts to do something like that. She blinked at Ry and Bram as they stood and offered their hands. Still dizzy from the orgasm, she curled her fingers over theirs and let them help her to her feet. She was grateful to have them to hold on to as she stepped down from the wagon, otherwise there was a good chance she would have ended up sprawled face first on the snow-covered parking lot. Talk about a potential embarrassment. Her knees shaky, she leaned against the side of the wood railing, too satiated by her climax to care that she was probably wearing the dopiest grin ever.

While Bram and Ry carted the spruce the short distance to the station where it would be tied up for easier transport, the driver tipped his wool cap to her and smiled, flashing some seriously bucked teeth. "Come again now."

Somehow she stifled a giggle and instead kept a straight face as she repeated Ry's earlier sentiment. "Believe me, that's a given."

Up until that day, she couldn't recall Ry ever breaking any traffic laws. From the moment they left the tree farm and screeched into Bram's driveway, Ry broke at least ten. Not that she was counting. Or complaining, since the end result meant her being able to rip off their clothes that much sooner.

Ignoring the Christmas tree bundled and waiting in the bed of the pickup truck, Ry and Bram hustled her from the vehicle and inside the warm comfort of the house. Bram tugged her coat from her while Ry worked on her jeans. Equally busy, she wrestled with their jackets. Clothes went flying everywhere. With each inch of skin revealed, her hunger for both men quadrupled. Her fingertips skated over washboard abs, grazed over hard, masculine nipples. She trembled, the ache inside her overwhelming. Finally everyone was blessedly naked, and she dropped to her knees and reached for the thick, stiff cocks bobbing in front of her.

The only thought in her mind was giving them even a fraction of the intense pleasure they'd shown her in the tree wagon. Delirious with that need, she sucked Ry into her mouth first, her tongue coasting along each rigid vein before swirling over the swollen head. She reveled in his taste. So addictive. So divine. *So good.* She pumped Bram's shaft, keeping it nice and firm for when she'd take him inside her mouth. The groans tumbling from both men only spurred her desire to see them fly off the edge.

Transferring her attention to Bram, she bobbed

frantically on his cock, her cheeks hollowing as she concentrated on the taut, satiny head. He staggered, his fingers sifting through her hair. "Lace...*God.*"

Her suction intensified and Bram quickly disengaged from her mouth. Shifting her focus to Ry, she attempted to lick the drop of precome pearling from the slit of his cock, but he thwarted her efforts by stooping and sweeping her into his arms. Without saying a word, he carried her into the bedroom and tossed her onto the mattress. The carnal, almost predatory gleam in his eyes brought a renewed surge of moisture between her legs.

She'd thought she'd seen Ry at his most primal. That didn't hold a candle to the possessive, sexy man leaning over her. Fisting his shaft, he held it to her lips. "Five seconds, baby. That's all you're getting before I bury myself inside you."

Intent on spending her time wisely, she gripped Ry's knuckles and squeezed as she flicked her tongue over the glossy knob of his cock. The mattress dipped, announcing that Bram had joined them. His lips closed around her clit, sucking with soft, gentle pulses. She writhed, her pussy tightening around the bullet still lodged within her. Bram's fingers wedged inside her slick channel and easily slipped the vibrator free. "Christ, you're fucking wet, Lace. The bullet really worked you over."

Without warning, Ry wrenched himself from her mouth. She gasped in protest. "That wasn't five seconds."

"Close enough." A nerve ticking in his tensed jaw, Ry yanked the drawer open on the nightstand and snatched two condoms, one of which he passed to Bram.

After sheathing himself, Bram bracketed her face between his hands and crashed his mouth over hers, stealing her breath. And her last shred of sanity. His tongue plunged deep a fraction of a second before his cock followed suit. Giving her the barest moment to register his penetration, he rolled onto his back, reversing their positions. His hands tangled in her hair, holding her hostage to the continued lush invasion of his tongue inside her mouth. It was as if he wasn't merely kissing her. No, this was hunger at its most consuming peak.

Ry's knee nudged her and Bram's thighs, spreading them. An instant later, the heat of his chest blanketed her back. Sandwiched as she was between the two strong, sexy men who'd breathed her fantasies into life, she couldn't contain the shiver that trembled through her. Ry kissed her neck, stoking her pleasure higher. His cock slid along the crease of her ass before coming to rest at the juncture where she and Bram were already joined.

His thumb pressing down on Bram's shaft, Ry eased his way inside her pussy. A sharp intake of breath hissed between Bram's teeth. "*Jesus.*"

Dazed, she felt her channel stretching to accommodate both Ry and Bram. Impaled on so much cock, she shuddered, the overwhelming fullness threatening to make her climax without much effort on Ry and Bram's part. "*Oh. God.*"

Bram's gaze locked with hers, his gorgeous features a

study of agonized pleasure. "Lace. *Fuck.*"

"I—I don't think I can. Too tight to move."

His laugh gusted free, the sound hoarse and strained. "Shit, you're telling me."

Ry's bristly jaw buffed her cheek. "So you two are saying *I* have to do all the work? Typical." He flexed his hips, his cock retreating slightly before surging deeper. The friction against the sensitive walls of her pussy filled her with a dark, decadent pleasure. The sensations skyrocketed when Ry straightened his arms, his fingers digging into the bedding as he balanced his weight, and slammed forward, grinding her and Bram into the mattress.

Bram's mouth went slack, his pupils dilating and becoming unfocused. Tiny beads of sweat dotted his forehead. The tortured sound that tore from his chest made her nipples tighten.

"Not..." Ry pumped once, "...before..." twice, "...Lacey." His third thrust pinned them tight to the mattress again.

Bram's pleading gaze bore into hers. It was all the invitation her body needed to explode. She arched with a strangled scream, her inner muscles clamping down on the two cocks buried deep within her. The emotional avalanche decimated her, reducing her to a sobbing, quivering wreck. It wasn't until the raw, scratchiness of her throat became noticeable that she even recognized the fact that her screams had morphed into actual words.

Words that even then were spinning in the air with horrible, alarming clarity. "I love you. Oh God, I love you."

The echoing shouts of completion from Bram and Ry hardly drowned out her damning confession.

CHAPTER FOURTEEN

Her heart thundering, she rolled off Bram the second Ry dismounted. She started to jump off the bed, but Bram's fingers cuffed her wrist, stalling her short.

"Lace, look at me."

Despite every internal defense mechanism warning her not to do it, she obeyed his soft command. His eyes held an overflow of tenderness. "Don't be freaked out because of what you admitted. We love you too. Have for a long time."

His unexpected words hammered into her. Pulse speeding out of control, she jerked her gaze to Ry, who was watching her with an expression identical to Bram's. "*What?*"

"That's right, baby. We've been madly, hopelessly in love with you for going on damn near fifteen years."

"But..." The panic bells began tolling in her head. "You never said anything. Never so much as hinted..." Her eyes narrowed. "You were going to let me marry Dan." And look where that had gotten her. Further proof that love was only a heartache she couldn't afford.

Ry and Bram both grimaced, but it was Bram who ultimately addressed her accusation. "If we'd known what a cheating prick he was, we would never have let you go out with him in the first place."

She plunked her hands on her hips. "*Let* me go out with him?"

Bram's cheeks reddened. "Shit, that didn't come out right."

Ry scooted off the mattress and walked toward her. "What Bram's trying to say is that we wanted you to be happy. Obviously Dan didn't feel the same way. But we can change all that now. You, Bram and I, we can forge our happiness together."

Like a taunting ghost that'd been waiting for the perfect moment to feed her insecurities, Olivia's voice popped inside Lacey's head. *You know why Dan left, don't you? Because you're boring. A goody-goody who doesn't know the first thing about how to please a man. Or keep him happy. Or should we say keep him period?*

Ry moved to hug her, but she stumbled out of his reach and hurried down the hallway. She could hear him and Bram following after her, but she forced herself not to look at them as she stopped in the entryway and tugged on her jeans.

"Baby, what are you doing?"

She pulled on her sweater, despising the way her fingers shook. "Going home."

"Why?"

"Because I can't be here right now." Not when the walls were closing in on her and she felt like she was seconds away from throwing up.

Before she could stop him, Bram stepped in front of the door, blocking her exit. "Whatever's scaring you, Lace, don't listen to it. We're here for you." He cupped her face, forcing her to meet the sincerity in his gaze. "Always."

"Please, I—I just need to be by myself for a while."

Ry's hands settled on her shoulders. "Don't shut us out, baby. Not now. Not after everything we've been through."

She swallowed, the agitation sticking in her throat. "I told you this would end up being a mistake."

A flash of pain flickered in Bram's eyes. "Don't say that. Loving each other isn't a mistake."

"It will be when this doesn't work out. And how can it? For God's sake, Bram, there are three of us in this equation. Not exactly the norm."

"We'll figure it out. Hell, it's not like this place isn't big enough for all of us."

She gaped at him. His Adam's apple bobbed. "Or...we can move into your place. I'm not averse to selling my house. And Ry's lease is almost up on his condo."

Danger. Danger. Danger. This was how it all started. Talk of a future that would ultimately crumble into shattered illusions. She'd been down this road before and recognized a devastating oncoming collision when she saw one. "No one is moving anywhere." Jerking out of Bram's and Ry's grasps, she bent and swiped her purse from where it'd landed earlier. Straightening, she sent Bram a resolute stare while inside she trembled. "Don't make me beg you to step away from the door."

Bram's face fell. "Lace—"

"Let her go."

Bram glanced at Ry in surprise. Taking advantage of his distraction, she scooted under the arm he had braced on the doorframe and reached for the knob.

Ry's voice wrapped around her with tenderness. "Baby, we love you. Just remember that."

She stumbled out the door. Halfway to her car, she realized why she was shivering spastically. She'd left her coat back in the house. Not even chilled bones would convince her to risk repeating the painful scene she'd just left. Stomach lurching, she jumped in her Pathfinder and somehow worked her shaking fingers enough to fumble the key into the ignition and steer the vehicle out of the driveway.

The real miracle was keeping down her breakfast until she made it home to her bathroom.

CHAPTER FIFTEEN

Sitting through a second grade Christmas pageant with a heavy heart and an awful sickness churning in her stomach wasn't exactly Lacey's idea of a good time. Unfortunately, she didn't have much choice but to grin and bear it since she'd promised her aunt Eliza weeks ago that she wouldn't miss Jamie's big debut as one of Santa's elves. Being a single parent, Eliza counted on all the family support she could get. And with Lacey's parents already down in Florida, Lacey was pretty much all Eliza and Jamie had. She couldn't let them down.

Somehow she managed to smile and clap when her niece and the rest of the eight year olds took their bows before giggling and scurrying toward the auditorium wings of Hofferton's Elementary School. Clutching her purse like a lifeline, Lacey turned toward her aunt with a smile that she prayed didn't look half as pained as it felt. "Well, give Jamie a big kiss for me and tell her I think we have a star in the making."

Aunt Eliza's lips hitched into a frown. "I thought you were joining us for dinner."

"Thanks, but if you don't mind, I think I'll skip it this time. All the hours I've been putting in at the restaurant have really tuckered me out the past few days." That and trying to cope with the turmoil inside her heart.

"But, hon, it's the holidays. Plus I know how much Jamie would love getting to have her most favoritest person in the whole world brag on her performance."

The woman was a freaking pro at wheedling people into going along with her plans. Lacey sighed softly. "All right, count me in."

"Fantastic!" Eliza hugged Lacey tight, enveloping her in a gardenia-scented cloud. The strong potency of her aunt's perfume increased Lacey's queasiness.

"I'll follow you guys. Where do you want to go?"

"Well, I did promise Jamie she could have one of those Shirley Temples that your bartender George makes special for her."

Great. As if seeing Ry and Bram twelve hours a day and dodging their pleas to come back wasn't enough to deal with, now she'd have to face them with family looking on and pretend that her world wasn't spinning out of control. "Sounds like a plan, then. I'll meet you there in a few."

After giving her aunt a kiss, she ducked out of the auditorium and hurried across the school parking lot to her car. Once inside the cold vehicle, she pressed her forehead against the steering wheel and gulped past the misery congealing in her windpipe.

How the hell had everything turned so wrong?

She'd known giving in to her desire for her two best friends would backfire on her. It was only supposed to be a fun, sexy affair. That she could handle. Love, on the other hand, was something she couldn't afford to give away. Just thinking about it tightened the ball of tension riding against her sternum.

She'd never survive it if Ry and Bram decided they didn't want to be with her. Unlike Dan, she knew they wouldn't try to get out of the relationship by cheating on her. No, they were too good and honorable for that. And somehow that made it worse. They wouldn't give her an easy out. Wouldn't commit a despicable act that would make it easy to hate them in the end. No, they wouldn't do anything. That was the problem. Rather than hurt her, they'd stay in a relationship that they might not want.

A wash of acid burned her throat. It was better to be practical about this and end things now, while their friendship still remained. Ry and Bram might not see things the same way she did, but when they moved on with their individual lives and found the right women to start families with, they'd realize this threesome couldn't have worked.

She tried not to let the idea of Ry and Bram marrying other women and settling down bother her. Why should it? She wanted them to be happy, to lead fulfilling lives filled with a surplus of love. They both deserved it. So, so much.

Her throat constricting, she lifted her head from the steering wheel and started up the car. Less than fifteen minutes later, she pulled into the Dockside's parking lot. With it being less than a week away from Christmas, the restaurant was at nearly full capacity.

Good. Hopefully it meant Ry and Bram would be too busy to continue their constant quest to lure her back into their arms.

Right. As if she stood any chance of that not happening. Steeling her spine, she sucked in a deep, steadying breath and pushed open her car door. She made it inside the restaurant just as the first new flurries of snow began swirling from the darkening sky. Unwinding the scarf from her neck, she scanned the dining room for sign of her aunt and niece. Her heart plummeted when she spotted Ry and Bram standing at Eliza and Jamie's table.

So much for that.

Her steps sluggish, she started toward them. Bram said something to Jamie before tweaking her long blonde braid. The young girl beamed up at him, her gap-toothed smile a mile wide. The cramping in Lacey's chest intensified. Bram was so amazing with kids, as was Ry. They were well suited for fatherhood.

Didn't they see what they'd be missing out on if they continued this three-wheeled relationship? She'd be selfish to deprive them of that.

Ry looked up then and noticed her. His eyes were lined with fatigue. Her heart twisted, knowing that in all likelihood, she was a large portion of the reason for his sleepless nights. She swallowed and curled her fingers against her palms to resist stroking his dear face.

"There you are, hon." Aunt Eliza finished shrugging from her massive down coat before taking a seat. "Would you please tell your men to stop looking so gorgeous? It's going to give a woman ideas."

Tell me about it. She chose to ignore Eliza's remark, as well as the way she'd referred to Ry and Bram as Lacey's men. Yeah, best not to allow her mind to dwell on that futile thought. Instead she settled her purse on the table and adopted a bland expression as she glanced between Ry and Bram. "I'm surprised to see you guys still here. I thought you weren't working the night shift."

"We're not," Ry answered, his dark, penetrating stare never leaving her face. "My cousins dropped off Charlie a few minutes ago. Bram and I were thinking of taking him to see that new action flick."

"Charlie's here?" Everything else fled her mind as she peered around the dining room.

"He's in my office," Ry said. "Did you want to say hi to him before we take off?"

She swallowed, the guilt surfacing that Ry had even felt compelled to ask. Before the fallout of their relationship, he would never have hesitated over such a simple thing. Hell, it probably would have been a given that she'd be tagging along with them to the movies. She hated that she'd caused this strain between them. "Of course."

Aunt Eliza looked up from the picture Jamie was scribbling on the paper tablecloth. "Why don't you boys and Uncle Charlie join us for dinner first? That's if you haven't eaten already."

Panic started to seize Lacey, but before she could open her mouth, Ry and Bram accepted Eliza's offer. While Ry went to fetch his uncle, Bram sidled next to Lacey. He stared at her with those pleading puppy-dog eyes, and her stomach clenched.

Why did he have to make this so much harder than it already was?

"How're you doing, Lace?"

"F-fine. The pageant was lovely. Thank you again for covering for me today." God, she sounded so stiff and formal. Would it always be like this from now on?

The sorrow that fell across Bram's face was unbearable to witness. Her heart feeling like it was ripping in two, she stepped around him and took the chair next to Jamie. A few minutes later, Ry showed up with Uncle Charlie. The older man's face lit up as soon as he spotted her.

Scooting back her seat, she stood and wrapped him in a tight hug. "Heya, Unks." Although they weren't blood relatives, she'd always treated him as such. Something that Charlie seemed to like. "It's good to see you."

"My stubborn nephew insisted I needed to get out." Despite the gruffness in his tone, a hint of gratefulness lurked in Charlie's eyes as he glanced at Ry and gave a wavering smile. It must be hard, even after all these years, to have had the love of his life taken away by cancer. She couldn't imagine what it must be like.

Aunt Eliza pulled out the seat next to her. "Park yourself over here next to me, Charlie. It's been a while since we've chatted."

As always, Eliza's persuasiveness wasn't to be denied, and Charlie dutifully complied. That left the chairs on either side of Lacey unoccupied.

But of course. Fate would have it no other way than to sandwich her between Ry and Bram when her emotions were running at an all-time low. They wedged in beside her, bombarding her with their nearness and the overwhelming allure of their presence. She struggled not to breathe in the dizzying maleness they exuded. Tried not to imagine their hands and mouths trekking across every inch of her skin.

A brief silence descended on the table, the only sound the scratching of Jamie's crayon as she drew a detailed depiction of Santa popping a wheelie on a bicycle. Eliza was busy digging around in her bag, hence her uncharacteristic muteness. Finally Charlie cleared his throat. "Carolyn would have liked this place."

Even without looking in Ry's direction, she sensed his surprise. It wasn't like Charlie to mention his wife during the holidays. Usually it was too painful for him.

"She always loved the lake, you know," Charlie continued. The wobble in his voice was barely discernable.

Another first. "We were going to use our retirement savings to go on a cruise. One of those two-week Mediterranean trips. It was all she could talk about."

Eliza set her purse aside and squeezed Charlie's wrinkled hand. "You should still go on that cruise. Carolyn would have wanted you to."

"Yeah, that she would." Charlie's eyes filled with tears. "Maybe I should do it. Life's too short to regret the things we let slip us by because it hurts too much to let go of the past."

His words settled with a heavy ache in the pit of her belly. Ry's and Bram's fingers brushed hers under the table. She could hear their silent pleas loud and clear.

Oh God. She couldn't do this. Gulping down the bitter remorse clogging her esophagus, she shoved back her seat and rushed from the table. She reached the ladies' room just as Ry's and Bram's arms tugged her into their embrace. Panicked desperation clawing within her, she pushed away from them. "Please, just let me go."

"Lace, that's impossible. We're in this for the long haul, don't you see that?"

"Don't do this to me. It's not fair."

Ry's palm smoothed along her cheekbone. "You know what's not fair? Running away because you're too afraid of getting hurt again. Charlie's right. At some point, you have to let go of the past, baby."

"Why can't you understand I'm doing what's best for all of us? You both deserve to get married. Have a family."

"What the hell do you think the three of us are?" Ry demanded.

"It's not the same."

"Fuck that. It's the only one that matters to me. Matters to Bram." The conviction in Ry's fierce gaze brought tears to her eyes.

Because she knew he was fooling himself, she said, "This conversation is done with. Please, don't make it any worse." Before either of them could stop her, she rushed inside the bathroom. Emotionally drained, she slumped against the tiled wall and cried.

CHAPTER SIXTEEN

Feeling like a sluggish zombie, Ry swiped the razorblade through the shaving cream lathered on his jaw. He couldn't bring himself to meet his own gaze. No doubt the hollowness there matched the emptiness residing in his chest.

His life was a fucking mess, and he didn't know what the hell to do to turn everything around. To make it right again.

No, strike that. He knew what he wanted, what he *needed* to feel whole again. But the one woman who completed him refused to give up her fears.

She'd said she loved him—something he'd dreamt of hearing his entire goddamned life. It was a bittersweet revelation.

He flicked on the faucet and rinsed the last traces of foam from his face before washing out the basin. The task was a mindless one, requiring minimal energy on his part.

Fortunate, since he felt completely dead inside.

He yanked on his jeans and a crewneck. Combed his hair. By the time he was finished going through the motions, the coffeemaker spat out the last of its cycle. He poured a cup and took a gulp, not really registering its taste. The hot liquid settled in his gut in an unpleasant way. He dumped the remainder down the drain and scooped his keys from the counter. During the elevator ride down to the main level of his condo complex, he stared at the flickering fluorescent bulb overhead that the maintenance staff kept forgetting to replace.

Why the hell did he continue to live in this damn place? He didn't even particularly like it.

His thoughts returned to Bram's suggestion of them all moving into his house. A fresh ache pierced his heart. He couldn't imagine a future that didn't include Lacey. Didn't include Bram.

He'd never felt this fucking alone. Not even when he'd run away as a kid and struggled to survive on his own. The streets might have toughened him, prepared him for life, but they'd never prepared him for this. To the rest of the world, he might still resemble the self-assured guy he struggled at portraying, but inside he was a mushy mess, pining for a woman and a life he would never have.

His motions listless, he cleared the light dusting of snow from the headlights of his truck before making the drive into work. The fortunate part about handling the afternoon shift was missing morning rush-hour traffic on Jefferson Avenue. Even that bit of good luck did nothing to lift his spirits. He pulled into his parking spot in front of the Dockside and killed the engine. Pocketing his keys, he made his way inside the restaurant.

A few of the regulars up at the bar called out greetings. Pasting on a smile, he shot a brief wave in their direction and crossed to his and Bram's office. He peeled off his coat and tossed it onto his chair. The door snicked open and he turned. His gaze locked with Lacey's startled one.

"Oh, sorry. I didn't realize…" Swallowing, she dropped her focus to the floor. Refusing to look at him, she hurried toward Bram's desk.

He stared at her while she dug through the small pile of invoices. It'd been five fucking days since she'd slammed the restroom door on him and Bram and left them reeling.

God, she was ripping his heart out. "We need to talk."

She glanced up at him, her expression wary. "I'm kind of busy right now." She gestured toward the invoice in her hand.

"That wasn't a request."

Her lips rolled into a tight line, but surprisingly she nodded. He zeroed in on her mouth, wanting with every fiber in his being to tug her into his arms and kiss some sense into her. If they were anywhere else but here, he would have. But he knew he was treading on perilous ice as it was. One false step and it'd crack right out from under him.

His life was in enough turmoil. He didn't need to sink

it further. "I've missed you, baby."

Her mouth trembled. "You see me every day."

"It's not the same. Do you know how hard it is to be this close to you and feel like you're miles away?"

"Would it be easier if I was?"

His stomach pitched, threatening to send up the coffee he'd choked down earlier. "What are you saying?"

"M-maybe it would be better for all of us if I sold my share of the Dockside."

It took two angry steps to reach her. Once he did, he gripped her shoulders, resisting the urge to shake her. "Don't talk fucking stupid shit like that to me, goddamn it."

She gulped. "I didn't mention it to make you mad, but I don't want this to end up something that could hurt the business. I wouldn't do that to you and Bram."

"No, you'll just stomp on our fucking hearts, that's all."

Tears gathered in her eyes. "I asked you not to make this worse than it already is."

"It's too late for that, baby. You and Bram, you're the two things in this world that have kept me going. Given me a reason to believe that my life is worth a shit." He eased his grip on her, but the tremor in his hands didn't lessen. "I can't remember a time I didn't love you. I used to think it was impossible for me to feel any more miserable, knowing I couldn't tell you what was inside my heart. But that doesn't begin to compare with what I'm going through now."

He let go of her and plowed his fingers through his

hair. "Hell, maybe you're the smart one. Locking out any chance of love and running in the opposite direction. Maybe if I'd done that, I wouldn't be slowly dying inside." Despite his best efforts to control it, his voice broke on the tail end of his statement. Worried he was seconds away from completely unmanning himself, he pivoted and strode from the office just as Bram stepped out of the stockroom carrying reels of receipt paper for the registers.

Bram halted, his expression worried. "What's going on?"

"She suggested selling her share of the business."

Bram's focus veered to the closed office door. "*What?*"

His mouth twisted with bitterness. "My words exactly. I told her there's no fucking way we're going along with that."

"Maybe I should talk to her."

"It won't do a damn bit of good," he bit out flatly. "She's never coming around."

He figured Bram's stricken features were a mirror of his own. He felt like the world's hugest bastard killing Bram's last hope, but it was a necessary evil.

They both needed to face the facts. Lacey might love them, but she was too afraid to ever allow them access to her heart.

Pain cramping her chest, Lacey stared at the door Ry had vacated only seconds before. She had the odd sensation that although she was standing in Ry and Bram's office, she might as well be a universe away from the comfortable world she used to know.

Charlie's words echoed with harsh recrimination inside her head. *Life's too short to regret the things we let slip us by because it hurts too much to let go of the past.*

Oh God. What the hell was she doing? Everything she'd ever wanted was outside that door. She'd sustained herself with the fantasy of Ry and Bram through the toughest time in her life, and now she was too afraid to go after the real thing?

Ry was right. She *was* a coward. The awful shame of it sat like a boulder in her stomach.

They'd been there for her. Always. And she was hurting them in a way that was worse than the betrayal she'd gone through with Dan.

Her heart squeezed and tears streamed down her cheeks unchecked. If there was one thing she'd come to realize, it was that running didn't do a damn bit of good. These past several days of barely surviving more than proved that fallacy.

So what the hell are you waiting for, you idiot?

A desperate sob hiccupping from her throat, she rushed toward the door. Those six steps felt like the longest of her life. She twisted the knob, banging her hip on it in her haste to open the door. Ignoring the burst of pain, she stumbled out into the bar area, looking around frantically.

She spotted Ry and Bram at the register installing receipt tape for George. Other than the four of them and the handful of customers situated at the bar and the neighboring booths, the room was relatively empty. Elvis was crooning about a blue Christmas on the restaurant's speakers. How fitting. She cleared her throat, praying it'd be heard over the music. It must have worked because every eye turned on her, including Ry's and Bram's. Their faces looked haggard. Resigned.

She'd done that to them. Time to make things right. "You're wrong. It's not better to lock yourself away from love." She stepped forward, her knees shaky. "I'm tired of being afraid."

Ry stared at her, a fraction of the dark clouds lifting from his eyes. "So what are you saying?"

She took a deep breath, expelled it slowly. "That I love you guys, and I want to make our relationship work."

George's jaw dropped and speculative whispers cropped up from a few of the nearby diners. Oh yeah, they were going to have a field day with this one. Oh well. Might as well make it extra juicy for them. "My house is too small for the three of us. Much better to move into Bram's." A twinge of uncertainty shuttled through her. "That's if the offer is still open."

Ry and Bram practically leapt over the bar in their haste to reach her. Bram got to her first. He swung her into his arms and planted a hungry kiss on her that pretty much cleared up anyone's doubts regarding which direction their relationship swung. Bram pulled back, his expression joyous. "It's definitely still open. In fact, I think we should go get you packed right now."

She gave a sniffly chuckle. "We can wait until tomorrow. I'm not going anywhere."

Ry cupped the back of her head, his eyes flashing a tender fierceness. "Promise?"

She nodded. He leaned in, his lips brushing hers softly. "We'll make this work. We're the three amigos. Together, we can conquer anything." His voice held undeniable conviction.

"I love you both. So much." She stroked Ry's and Bram's faces, the emotion inside her chest no longer terrifying, but freeing.

"Hearing that is the best Christmas present you could have ever given me, baby."

"Me too, Lace."

She gave them both hopeful smiles. "So does this mean I'm saved from having to sing naked karaoke?"

Ry and Bram glanced at each other, their expressions thoughtful. After a silent debate they both pressed their mouths to her ears and whispered, "Not a chance."

She feigned a sigh. Really, she couldn't complain. When it came to helping a girl mark off her naughty list and teaching her to love again, her boys had been more than accommodating. Besides, she had every intention of making sure they performed their own naked karaoke.

Hey, fair was only fair.

About the Author

At the ripe age of seven, Jodi Redford penned her first epic, complete with stick-figure illustrations. Sadly, her drawing skills haven't improved much, but her love of fantasy worlds never went away. These days she writes about fairies, ghosts and other supernatural creatures, only with considerably more heat.

She has won numerous contests, including The Golden Pen and Launching a Star.

When not writing or working the day job, she enjoys gardening and way too many reality-television shows.

She loves to hear from readers. You can email her at jodiredford@jodiredford.com and visit her online at **www.jodiredford.com**.

Other Titles

Make Mine A Menage

The Naughty List
Checking It Twice

Kinky Chronicles

Perfect Chemistry
Kinky Claus
Report For Booty
Kinky Curves
Cowboy Kinky
Frisky Business

The Sons of Dusty Walker

Dylan

Zoe & Dylan

That Old Black Magic

That Voodoo You Do

The Seven Year Witch

Maximum Witch

Getting Familiar with Your Demon

Kissin' Hell

Thieves of Aurion

Lover Enslaved

Lover Enraptured

Also Available

Knotty Magic

Double Dare

Hurricanes and Handcuffs

Sweet Sizzle

Naughty Girls Do

Light My Fire

Vanessa Unveiled
Cat Scratch Fever
Breaking Bad
Three Ways to Wicked

Coming Soon

Bad Boys Do It Better
Triple Knockout
Double Dirty
Fakefully Yours

PERFECT CHEMISTRY

Leo Martinez and Devlin Hawke—the hottest geeks on the planet. And Sidney Chase's biggest weakness. Giving in to her secret fantasies about her sex-on-a-stick bosses? Out of the question. Until the night she's accidentally exposed to the supercharged aphrodisiac in their lab...

Despite their mutual craving for Sidney, Leo and Devlin consider her off limits. The last thing they'd wanted was to scare off their best PA by overwhelming her with their kinky tendencies. Witnessing the arousing effects of their aphrodisiac elixir on Sidney changes everything. Not only is she the answer they've been looking for in regards to fine-tuning their formula, she's the perfect woman for *them*. And with a little help from one helluva sinful science experiment, they'll prove that love is far more potent than anything manufactured in a bottle.

Warning: This red hot office romance contains 3 parts sizzling m/f/m menage, 2 parts sexy and sweet geeks, one part wicked bondage and sex toys, and a whole lot of combustible chemistry. Safety glasses required.

Devlin grabbed his coffee mug and crossed over to his office. He powered on his tablet and scrolled through his emails. Nothing much exciting beyond a few tech newsletters he subscribed to and an ad for penis enlargement. He deleted that one and settled in to peruse the article on 3-D printing. Halfway through his read he was hit with the odd certainty that something was off about the placement of his paperclip dispenser. Frowning, he leaned back in his chair. "Hey, were you messing with my stuff?"

A grunt came from the other side of the wall. "Yes, because clearly I have nothing better to do than drive your OCD ass crazy."

"Well, you are a maniacal motherfucker." Devlin made a point of loudly plopping the dispenser back into its proper position. "And it's not OCD. I use the stapler more often, so it should be front and center, not the paperclips."

"Admitting you have a problem is the first step in recovery."

"Asshole." Chuckling, Devlin finished up his coffee and returned to the kitchenette for a refill. He was waylaid on the round trip to his office with Leo's request to fetch his reading glasses from the lab. After tossing out a few teasing digs about his partner becoming an old man, Devlin made tracks down the hall and fished his badge from his pants pocket.

The moment he stepped into the lab he was struck once again with the peculiar sensation that something wasn't quite right. As much time as he spent in the space, it was practically his second home. So with that said, if his Spidey-sense was telling him that a detail wasn't as it should be, he was damn well going to listen up.

Rubbing his chin, he surveyed the room, mentally checking off boxes as he cataloged each detail individually. Trash can in corner—normal. Lab coats on their proper hooks? Yep. Workstations prepped and ready for—

His mental inspection skidding to a halt, he stared at the empty test tube holder resting on the station across from him. The vial had most definitely been there when he and Leo locked up yesterday.

So where the hell did it go?

Determined to get to the bottom of that mystery, he retraced his steps to Leo's office. "Did you do something with one of the vials from batch 39?"

Leo tore his focus from his monitor, his brow furrowed. "No. Why?"

"It's missing."

"What?"

Well aware of where Leo's thoughts were jumping, Devlin shot up his hand. "Don't burst your coronary. We don't know that this is a repeat of Texon." But after having one of their prized formula's ripped off by a competitor several years ago, the fear was there of it happening again. Even with all the precautions they'd taken to prevent a reoccurrence, the threat was always present. There was only so much they could do.

Leo vaulted from his chair and rushed from his office.

Devlin stayed hot on his heels. Once inside the lab, Leo confirmed Devlin's suspicions with a string of colorful obscenities. Raking his fingers through his hair, he shot a narrow squint at the panel obscuring the security camera in the corner. "Let's pray they were too sloppy to cover their ass."

What were the chances someone would be foolish enough to stroll in here and steal Xtacy without disguising their identity? Wisely deciding to keep that woeful dose of reality to himself, he followed Leo back to his office. With a quick click of his mouse Leo pulled up the link to the security system and located the time stamp for last night. He fast-forwarded through an hour or so of uneventful footage before a blip of motion flashed across the screen.

Leo's features hardened. "Got the son of a bitch." He rewound a few frames and pressed play.

On the footage, the lab lights flickered on and a woman stepped into view. Devlin blinked. "Wait a minute. Isn't that—?"

"Sidney." Her name fell from Leo with the same amount of bemusement that plagued Devlin. They both leaned closer to the computer as she sashayed to the workstation and picked up the test tube.

Devlin shook his head. "I don't believe it. Not of Sidney. No fucking way."

"Then what the hell are we looking at?" Leo demanded, his tone flatter than a desert highway. Despite the lack of inflection in his voice, Devlin knew his friend was hiding a world of hurt while he processed the visual evidence of Sidney's potentially traitorous activity.

"I don't know, but let's not jump to conclusions yet." *Come on, Sid. What are you doing?* His heart knocking, he waited for the moment she'd put the vial back and scurry out of there, completely unaware of the real criminal lurking in the shadows about to abscond with the Xtacy formula. The wish was a desperate shot in the dark on his part, but he refused to give up hope. No matter how thin it was. When the test tube went flying out of Sidney's grasp and smashed onto the floor, he straightened with a jolt, renewed optimism crashing over him. "She dropped it. *That's* why it's missing."

A fraction of the doubt lifted from Leo's gaze but his shoulders remained tense. "It still doesn't explain what in the devil she's doing in the lab."

"Who knows? Maybe she was just curious—" Devlin broke off abruptly when Sidney ripped off her blouse and wrenched down her bra. All coherent thought beating a hasty retreat from his head, he stared at the sheer magnificence of her breasts. She cupped their bountiful weight and tweaked her nipples. The real estate in Devlin's briefs suddenly became a lot more cramped. Gripping the edge of the desk, he risked a quick peek in Leo's direction and noticed his friend was equally enamored with the unexpected show.

Leo swallowed hard, his Adam's Apple bobbing. "We probably shouldn't watch any more of this."

"Yeah, we shouldn't."

They both kept their attention fused to the screen. Sidney's hand crept inside her panties. He and Leo adjusted their flies simultaneously. She bit her lip, her head falling back against the side of the workstation as her hips moved in rhythm to the motion of her fingers. Even with that miniscule scrap of fabric concealing the view, the sight playing out in front of them was tantalizing as fuck. She was completely uninhibited in her wild chase to the Big O finish line. The continued reel of her gasps and moans sizzled along Devlin's nerve endings, but it was his and Leo's names screamed at the top of her lungs when she ultimately came that sucker punched him like a two by four.

Holy shit. Jerking his gaze to Leo, Devlin discovered he wasn't the only one sledge hammered by that startling last part of her self lovin' session. "Uh, she just came while thinking about us." There was no denying the obvious. A person didn't just randomly scream someone's name at the height of passion.

Leo scrubbed a hand over his mouth, his wide-eyed stare still glued to his computer. "Fuck me."

"Uh, dude? Pretty sure that's *precisely* what she's saying."

CPSIA information can be obtained
at www.ICGtesting.com
Printed in the USA
BVHW030246161220
595834BV00017B/157